# ROBIN HOOD

## BALLOTS, BLASTS & BETRAYAL

Robert Muchamore's ROBIN HOOD series:

*1. Hacking, Heists & Flaming Arrows*
*2. Piracy, Paintballs & Zebras*
*3. Jet Skis, Swamps & Smugglers*
*4. Drones, Dams & Destruction*
*5. Ransoms, Raids & Revenge*
*6. Bandits, Dirt Bikes & Trash*
*7. Prisons, Parties & Powerboats*
*8. Ballots, Blasts & Betrayal*

Look out for more
ROBIN HOOD adventures, coming soon!

Other series by Robert Muchamore:

CHERUB
HENDERSON'S BOYS
ROCK WAR

Standalone novels by Robert Muchamore:

*KILLER T*
*ARCTIC ZOO*

# ROBERT MUCHAMORE'S
# ROBIN HOOD

## BALLOTS, BLASTS & BETRAYAL

HOT
KEY
BOOKS

First published in Great Britain in 2024 by
HOT KEY BOOKS
4th Floor, Victoria House, Bloomsbury Square
London WC1B 4DA
Owned by Bonnier Books
Sveavägen 56, Stockholm, Sweden
bonnierbooks.co.uk/HotKeyBooks

A CIP catalogue record for this book is available from the British Library.

ISBN: 978-1-4714-1343-8
*Also available as an ebook and in audio*

1

Typeset by DataConnection Ltd
Printed and bound in Great Britain by Clays Ltd, Elcograf S.p.A.

Hot Key Books is an imprint of Bonnier Books UK
bonnierbooks.co.uk

# ROBIN HOOD

# THE STORY SO FAR . . .

**Robin Hood** lived with his dad, **Ardagh**, and half-brother **Little John**, until his father got thrown in jail for a crime he didn't commit.

Robin's half-brother discovered that his mum was the wealthy businesswoman and politician **Marjorie Kovacevic** and went to live with her, while local gangster **Guy Gisborne** put a bounty on Robin's head, forcing him to hide out in Sherwood Forest and join a gang of righteous rebels led by **Emma** and **Will Scarlock**.

With his new rebel pals, Robin blew up cash machines, hacked computers, caused a massive flood, flipped a police car and busted his best friend **Marion Maid** out of prison.

The thirteen-year-old also became a social media sensation, with footage of his escapades getting millions of views.

# COMING NEXT . . .

Tomorrow is election day.

If Guy Gisborne is elected as the new Sheriff of Nottingham, he'll expand his brutal criminal empire across the county and into Sherwood Forest.

Nobody took Ardagh Hood seriously when he got out of jail and announced his rival bid to become sheriff. But Robin's dad has gained support from university students, rebels and locals who are sick of Gisborne's corruption.

Even though Gisborne funded a lavish advertising campaign, polls released on election eve show that the race to be the next Sheriff of Nottingham is too close to call.

Meanwhile, former sheriff Marjorie Kovacevic has used the run-up to election day to turn around her troubled attempt to become national president.

Thanks to a brilliant new campaign manager and gaffes by her opponent, Marjorie is hot favourite to become the next occupant of the Presidential Palace.

If she wins, Marjorie says she'll send soldiers and tanks into Sherwood, crushing the rebels and bringing the vast forest back under government control.

# 1. THE CROWD GOES WILD

21:01, ELECTION EVE

Being the world's most wanted thirteen-year-old can be a bore. Robin Hood had spent forty minutes hiding in a cobwebbed room, with several dead mice, a rusty cinema projector and his best friend Marion Maid.

'It's getting packed down in the hall,' said Marion, peering through a narrow projection slot that gave the room its only light.

'AHHHH . . .' Robin inhaled, then buried his nose in the sleeve of his hoodie to muffle a sneeze. 'The dust in here's getting right up my nose. We were only supposed to be here for five minutes.'

Marion ignored Robin's whingeing and kept looking down into the giant space thirty metres below. The building was still called 'the cinema' on maps of Locksley University, but its screen and seats had been stripped years ago, leaving an open space, used for stuff like exams and end-of-term parties.

On a wall that still bore the dirty outline of a cinema screen, a banner read:

**YOUR VOTE COUNTS – REGISTER NOW!**

More detailed signs explained that anyone aged eighteen or over who'd not yet registered could queue at one of a dozen desks, fill in a form and claim their right to vote in the following day's election.

But most of the students packing the hall hadn't suddenly fallen in love with democracy. They were at the voter registration drive because they'd heard rumours that Robin Hood and Marion Maid were going to make a headline-grabbing appearance.

Nobody in the crowd had seen Robin and Marion being sneaked in, but the presence of journalists, TV crews and vloggers convinced people that there would be something worth seeing if they stuck around.

Some in the crowd had doubts: Marion Maid had only escaped from prison a couple of weeks earlier and the bounty on Robin's head had just been upped to a million pounds. Why risk making a high-profile appearance in the heart of their enemy Guy Gisborne's territory?

But with polls showing the race to become Sheriff of Nottingham on a knife-edge, Ardagh Hood's campaign team hoped that a dramatic appearance by Robin and Marion under the nose of Locksley's corrupt police department might create a social media buzz among the kind of young voters that they needed to win over.

As Robin sneezed again, the projection room's door creaked open. Rebel security officer Azeem Nasri stepped in, wearing body armour and with a stun gun and pistol strapped to her belt. She was followed by Ten Man Eric, whose mountainous presence would hopefully discourage anyone from getting too close to Robin and Marion

'It's go time,' Azeem said, smiling guardedly. 'Have you two memorised the alternative escape routes?'

'Watched your walk-through videos twice,' Marion confirmed.

As Marion and Robin moved out of the projection room onto a tight set of spiral stairs, Ten Man gave the rope harnesses on the teenagers' backs a tug, making sure they were properly fitted.

'And you learned your speech?' Azeem asked Robin as she led the quartet down the stairs.

'Bit late if I didn't,' Robin quipped.

After four flights of stairs, they crossed through an abandoned staff locker room. The lights in the main auditorium had just been dimmed, and when Robin and Marion stepped in, a trumpet fanfare came over the PA system. A roar rose from the crowd and a spotlight swung around, blinding the pair of them.

'Good evening, all genders,' a young person announced over a PA. 'For one night only, I give you Marion Maid and Robin Hood!'

Rebel security was taking no chances. As Robin's eyes adjusted to the light, he saw a line of armed rebels on either side and at least two snipers up on the former cinema's balcony. To his left, a carefully picked mix of TV and online news crews had been allowed to get close, while in front eager students surged towards the metal barriers for a better look.

A green-haired student organiser handed Robin a microphone.

'Y'all having fun?' Robin shouted, managing to sound more confident than he felt. 'I can't stay long, because Marion and I have had one or two recent legal difficulties.'

Robin paused as the jostling students laughed, cheered and recorded on their phones.

'I wanted to drop by to tell you to register to vote. Then vote for my dad, Ardagh Hood!'

A more muted cheer went up.

'We can't let Guy Gisborne keep wrecking this town, ripping off students in his dodgy nightclubs and flooding the poorest neighbourhoods in Locksley with drugs. And we can't let someone like Marjorie become president, to send tanks into Sherwood to kill or lock up thousands of innocent people.

'I always thought politics was boring, but this election matters. If you've got friends who haven't registered to vote, hit them up and tell them to get their butts down here by midnight. And tomorrow, go and vote to make *your* town and *your* country a better place.'

As Robin spoke, Marion moved closer to the crowd barriers, where people reached out, grasping her hoodie and begging for selfies and autographs.

'Why me?' Marion said, looking baffled.

'You're as famous as Robin since you busted out of jail,' one student yelled.

'You rule,' another added. 'Girl power!'

After Robin did a mic drop, lights flashed and pounding music came out of the PA system as he joined Marion at the barriers for selfies and autographs.

Ten Man leaned between them and spoke firmly. 'We've kept the cops out, but you've got ninety seconds before we have to get out of here.'

Robin had his selfie taken with a woman in a sombrero who smelled of rum, signed two T-shirts, posed for selfies, and had milkshake splashed on his hoodie by a guy who tried to pull him over the barrier for a hug. Marion had a similar experience, but looked less comfortable since it was her first brush with fame.

'Robin, I'm a reporter from the *Daily Courier*,' a grey-haired woman said as she pushed between students while videoing on her phone. 'We're running an interview with the wife of the prison guard you *murdered* in tomorrow's paper. Is there anything you'd like to say to the grieving widow and her nine-year-old son?'

The *Courier* was a notoriously pro-Marjorie, anti-rebel newspaper. A burly student shoved the journalist away and growled, 'I wouldn't wipe my crack on your newspaper. Get out of here!'

As the *Courier* journalist stumbled back and got hissed at by a couple of Robin's fans she yelled, 'Read my article, Robin. It's just gone live on the *Courier* website.'

Robin was startled, but managed to stay composed for a couple more selfies. Then he waved to the TV cameras as Ten Man grabbed Robin's rope harness and tugged him back from the barrier.

'Time to fly,' Ten Man said, as he hooked a rope that had just dropped from the ceiling to Robin's harness.

'You OK?' Robin asked, glancing at Marion while Ten Man clipped a second rope to her harness.

Marion smiled awkwardly. 'Probably the weirdest minutes of my life.'

It got weirder. Ten Man gave a double thumbs up to a pulley operator in an overhead lighting gantry. As the crowd of students went nuts, the rope jerked Marion and Robin off the ground and zipped them towards the ceiling.

'Vote Ardagh!' Robin shouted, making victory signs with both hands as he rose up.

The pair stepped onto the narrow metal gantry, and security officer Azeem and her sister Lyla helped them remove their harnesses.

'Up the ladder, over the roof and down the fire escape,' Azeem told them firmly. 'Ísbjörg's waiting for you in the getaway car.'

# 2. OUR ONCE GREAT COUNTRY

21:19

Lyla handed Robin a pack with his bow sticking out of the back and gave him a gentle thump on the shoulder. Then Marion pulled herself up through the hatch in the cinema's moonlit roof.

'Your speech was great,' she said. 'The crowd was eating out of your hands.'

A gust of wind swept rain into Robin's face as he jogged over a flat section of roof then got a wet bum as he followed Marion, sliding down sloping tiles to a gutter at the roof's edge. Next, they had to straddle the streaming gutter and make a three-metre drop onto a fire escape.

'Want me to lower you down?' Robin asked, wiping rain out of his eyes as Marion hesitated.

Marion's instinct was to scowl and insist she could manage. Then she glanced down at the drop, and the rain blasting the narrow fire escape, close to a railing with spiked strips to deter birds.

'This drop looked easier in Azeem's escape video,' she admitted. 'In daylight.'

Robin squatted down with one boot in the gutter, gripped a ventilation pipe with one hand, then let Marion take the other.

'Can you lower me with one arm?' she quizzed.

Robin was small, but he lifted weights and was crazy strong. Marion was impressed when Robin lowered her and her backpack down to the fire escape, with one arm and no sign of strain.

'All good?' Robin asked, then let Marion drop the last half-metre down to the rusting gantry.

'Good,' Marion confirmed, as her boots clanked on the metal floor.

There was a short ladder decorated with bird poop, then a more substantial outdoor staircase, built to allow hundreds of patrons out of the upper balcony after a film. But as Robin swung his legs out over the gutter and prepared to jump, a garbled message came from the walkie-talkie zipped inside his sodden hoodie.

'We didn't catch that,' Marion said into her own radio.

They both recognised the voice of Ísbjörg, the young rebel security officer who was supposed to be their getaway driver.

'Robin, Marion, don't come down here,' Ísbjörg repeated urgently. 'I've got cop cars blocking my exit and a panel van behind with nasty-looking dudes pouring out of the back.'

'Tits!' Robin gasped, looking down at Marion.

Marion spoke into her radio. 'Keep safe, Ísbjörg. Azeem, where shall we go?'

Azeem's voice came back over the radio. 'You two get back inside. We'll figure another way out.'

Robin gave Marion a worried look as he went full stretch to pull her back up to the roof. They held hands as they stumbled up the slippery roof tiles.

'We just got soaked for no reason,' Robin complained, as he dropped back through the roof hatch in front of Azeem. 'What now?'

Robin glanced over the lighting gantry and saw pushing and shoving down in the hall. Students screamed and bolted out of emergency exits, while a dozen thugs armed with cricket bats and metal bars had stormed the hall and begun to demolish the voter registration tables.

'I guess Gisborne reckons students aren't gonna vote for him,' noted Marion as she leaned over the gantry beside Robin.

They watched a bulky man in a puffa jacket pick up a folding table stacked with *Vote Ardagh* leaflets and roar as he hurled it towards the retreating students.

'You two stay put and keep out of sight,' Azeem ordered. 'I've got plenty of guys on the ground. We'll get you out of here somehow.'

As Azeem shot off to organise her security teams, Robin and Marion laughed as the thug who'd thrown the table got hit with a rebel officer's stun gun and spasmed on the floor like a fish out of water.

'Serves the dirtbag right,' Marion said, as she slid a compact crossbow from her backpack. 'You should get your bow out.' Then she was surprised to see Robin pulling out his phone and typing something.

'Hello? Earth to Robin? Can you stay offline for *ten* seconds?'

Robin ignored her and kept staring at his screen, waiting for something to load.

'Azeem told us to hide,' Robin said irritably. 'We don't know which escape routes are blocked, and if we shoot arrows from up here, those thugs down there will know we're still here.'

Marion saw no sign of cops entering the building, but the vanload of lightly armed thugs that Guy Gisborne had sent to stop students registering to vote hadn't expected a room containing two dozen rebel security officers.

'Gisborne's guys are getting battered,' Marion said happily.

'Uh-huh,' Robin mumbled.

Marion wanted to know what was distracting Robin from the giant screaming punch-up going on below. She spotted the red-and-white banner of the *Courier* newspaper on his screen and sighed.

'Don't believe *anything* on the *Courier* website. That newspaper is so biased. Marjorie could throw dynamite into a room full of bunnies and they'd still take her side.'

Robin didn't answer. His eyes were fixed on a headline that read:

**ROBIN HOOD MURDERED MY HERO HUSBAND**

Below the headline was a picture of a young man wearing a Pelican Island prison guard's uniform. A second picture showed the guard's wife and little boy, sitting on a sofa wearing black clothes and looking sad.

'This isn't *all* lies,' Robin said, sounding upset as he zoomed in on the picture of the guard. 'I remember that face. I shot him through the chest with an arrow while you were trying to escape.'

Marion rolled her eyes. 'He had an automatic rifle and a clear line of sight. If you hadn't shot him, he would have blasted me, Freya and all the others as we ran across that factory roof.'

'It still feels heavy,' Robin said with a sad shrug. 'I used the bow that's on my back right now to kill another human.'

'Don't be soft,' Marion said forcefully. 'Pelican Island guards are barely human. One time, they made my cousin Freya work a double laundry shift in high summer. When she fainted, the guards dragged her to the bathroom and made her drink water from a filthy toilet.'

'I'm not soft,' Robin growled, eyes still fixed on his phone. 'But I see that guy's face in my dreams. And people who read this article are gonna hate me.'

'People who read the *Courier* never liked you in the first place,' Marion pointed out. Then she read from the opinion box at the bottom of the article in a mocking voice, '"The *Courier* says it's time to get tough on welfare scroungers, rebels, immigrants and murderers like Robin Hood. Voting Marjorie Kovacevic for president could be our last chance to stop our once great country descending into anarchy." Seriously, Robin, you can't let drivel like this get you down.'

Ten Man's giant boots clanked on the end of the gantry before Robin could reply.

'Ísbjörg backed out and drove to the other side of the building,' Ten Man explained. 'Cops probably ignored her because she's young enough to pass for a student.'

'And Gisborne's people?' Robin asked.

'Thugs stormed in to bully students, and got the fright of their lives when they found twenty armed rebels.'

'So, we have a way out?' Marion asked.

'I'll escort you downstairs and out of a door at the back,' Ten Man explained. 'But we need to clear out fast. Gisborne will organise reinforcements, and we can't afford a shootout with his crew on their home turf.'

# 3. STRAWBERRY SOBS

21:56

Ardagh Hood's bid to become sheriff was being run out of a sprawling country mansion on Locksley's northern outskirts, which his campaign staff had nicknamed the White House.

The property was owned by Maud Newman, a Locksley-born entrepreneur who'd built a nationwide chain of noodle shops, but had been forced to leave her home town after refusing to pay Gisborne's violent thugs thousands of pounds a month in protection money.

Gisborne's bullying had turned Maud Newman into a wealthy enemy. As well as allowing Ardagh's campaign staff of Forest People, rebels and local activists to use her former home as a base, she'd provided IT equipment and tens of thousands in campaign funding.

The White House had the air of a fortress as two rebel security officers opened a high gate and let Ísbjörg roll onto the driveway in a Nissan SUV. Robin and Marion were half asleep in the back, while some of the security officers who'd been on guard at the cinema cruised behind in a pickup truck.

Robin felt safe inside the gates. Locksley's corrupt police force was understaffed and under-equipped, and Gisborne's thugs were better at bullying students and extorting money from local businesses than taking on a house protected by dozens of well-armed rebels.

Even if someone tried to attack the White House, there were storm drains to escape through and motorbikes on standby, enabling Robin to blast cross country and vanish into Sherwood Forest at the first hint of trouble.

'Nice evening's work, kid!' A long-limbed, paint-splattered dude named Gabriel shouted, fist-bumping Robin as he stepped out of the Nissan. Gabriel was a student dropout whose crew of stencil and graffiti artists had made it their mission to deface every one of Guy Gisborne's fancy advertising billboards.

'Gabes!' Marion said fondly, giving him a high five.

'Your high-wire escape is blowing up on social media,' Gabriel explained.

'Any TV?' Robin asked.

Gabriel checked the time on his phone. 'Ten o'clock news is about to start, so we'll see.'

Maud Newman's former home had a grand lobby with twin staircases, but after the six-week election campaign, there was trash everywhere and a lingering smell of stale takeaway food and people too busy to take showers.

As Robin crossed the lobby, he heard whirs and wooshes from a giant printer churning out neon campaign posters. To his right was an enormous lounge area, with random campaign staff sprawled over couches and pizza boxes stacked on a pool table.

'Pepperoni,' Robin said enthusiastically as he grabbed a hot slice and a can of Rage Cola.

Marion went for spicy vegan pizza and potato wedges. A woman in a yellow *Vote Ardagh* T-shirt took her socked feet off a sofa so there was room for them to sit.

'How come you smell of strawberry?' Marion asked, as she squeezed up next to Robin.

'It's the milkshake that nutter spilled all over me.'

Marion grinned. 'Beats your normal smell.'

Robin tutted as he reached towards the table to get potato wedges. 'You're *so* funny.'

The ten o'clock news began on a big screen at the far end of the room. The newsreader was Lynn Hoapili, who'd interviewed Robin for a TV special the year before. 'Here are the headlines on the eve of what some say are the most important elections for a generation . . .'

The first stories were about Marjorie and her rivals in the race for president, but the crowded lounge erupted in cheers as the screen cut to show Robin and Marion shooting into the air on ropes.

'Yesssss, you made national news!' the woman next to Robin screamed, then bounced so high she spilled Robin's can of drink.

'Maid and Hood made a risky and dramatic appearance at a voter registration drive earlier this evening,' Hoapili continued. 'But in other news, the *Courier* website has released an interview with the wife of a guard who claims that Robin murdered her husband during last month's dramatic escape from Pelican Island prison.'

Boos and shouts of 'No!' and 'Biased!' erupted around the lounge. A security officer threw a slice of pizza at the screen. It was a perfect shot that left a trail of pizza sauce down the newsreader's cheek.

Marion laughed, but Robin jumped off the couch and headed for the stairs.

'Damn.' Marion sighed, spilling potato wedges as she stood and went after her friend. 'Don't get upset, Robin. That's *exactly* what they want.'

Robin looked back at Marion as he reached the bottom of the stairs. 'But I did kill some little boy's dad, didn't I?'

'You had no choice,' Marion yelled, following him up the curved staircase.

Ísbjörg had also seen that Robin was upset, and ran a few steps behind.

Robin had a sleeping bag in a bedroom on the first floor. He planned to tell Marion to leave him alone and slam the door, but three little kids were sleeping on a bed by the window and his dramatic gesture would have woken them up and caused chaos.

Robin spun back into the hallway and stepped around Marion. Ísbjörg saw a tear streaking down Robin's face as she stuck her arms out to block his path.

'Don't run away,' Ísbjörg said firmly. 'You need to talk this through.'

Robin tried to duck under Ísbjörg's arms, but rebel leader Emma Scarlock had stepped out of her office and stood behind her. He thought about barging everyone out of the way, but instead Emma grabbed his arm and pulled him into a hug. Robin sniffed.

'Let it out, pal,' Emma said, as she held Robin tight and felt him sob. 'You're sad because you're a good person who has a conscience.'

'I killed that little boy's dad.' Robin sobbed as Emma rubbed his back. 'Maybe the guard was a bad person, but his family still loved him.'

'I know, I know,' Emma soothed, as she wondered why Robin smelled of strawberries.

'I can't believe I flipped out in front of everyone downstairs. I'm such an *idiot*.'

'No, you're not,' Marion said firmly.

'You inspire thousands of people,' Ísbjörg added.

'You're overtired,' Emma said, freeing Robin from the hug. 'There's nobody in the big bedroom at the end of the hallway. Freshen up in the shower then get some sleep, and you'll feel better in the morning.'

'I hope,' Robin said, managing half a smile as he wiped his eyes on his sleeve and backed up towards the end of the corridor.

# 4. FRUITY FRIDGE ART

04:45 ELECTION DAY

Robin crashed the instant his head hit the pillow. He woke just before 5am in the big bedroom and saw that a gently snoring Marion and two of her little brothers had joined him on the oversized bed.

He needed to pee and stumbled to the en-suite toilet, but a stench hit him when he opened the door.

'Nasty,' he gasped, backing out, gagging, after glancing at the mass of soggy toilet paper – and worse stuff he didn't want to think about.

Robin was only wearing briefs, so he grabbed a hoodie off the floor before stepping barefoot into the hallway, careful not to wake Marion or her bratty brothers.

Clearly nobody was cleaning the house, but Robin did find a slightly less disgusting toilet. As he peed, he realised he'd picked Marion's daisy-patterned hoodie off the dark bedroom floor.

Part of him wanted to snuggle back in bed, but it was noisy and all the lights were on downstairs. Several dozen campaign volunteers stood in the lobby dressed in outdoor clothes and a stream of people filtered through the kitchen, emerging with bacon rolls and hot coffee.

He recognised Ísbjörg's voice wafting out of the living room. 'We have twelve campaign buses,' she announced. 'We want at least two people handing out leaflets and encouraging people to vote for Ardagh outside every polling station.

'Keep safe. If you're harassed by cops or threatened by Gisborne's hoodlums, back off to avoid a confrontation and call the Rebel Control hotline if you need back-up. The first bus leaves in ten minutes and is heading towards the villages south of Nottingham. The second bus will—'

As Ísbjörg reeled off more bus routes and campaign stops, Robin decided to snatch a bacon roll before heading back to bed. But at the top of the stairs, he heard a gentle voice coming out of Emma Scarlock's office.

Robin knocked on the door and rebel leader Will Scarlock answered impatiently. 'We're in a meeting. Is it important?'

'Oh, no worries,' Robin said, but as he turned away from the door Will opened it and apologised.

'Robin, I didn't realise it was you. Come in, come in!'

Robin saw his dad in a leather armchair on the far side of a messy office papered with neon campaign posters. Since Robin was a fugitive and Ardagh was running for sheriff, they couldn't be seen together in public. And Ardagh had been campaigning all over the county in the last few weeks, so they'd barely seen each other in private either.

'I thought I heard your voice when I walked by,' Robin explained, noticing his father's neatly trimmed beard and ink-blue suit. 'Smart threads. You look like a proper politician!'

Ardagh's expression suggested he'd rather be in his usual jeans and baggy jumper as he stood up to give his son a hug.

'I heard you were upset last night,' Ardagh said.

'Woke up feeling better,' Robin said, smiling uneasily. 'Mostly, anyway.'

'I'll start worrying when you shoot a man and *don't* feel bad about it,' Ardagh said.

Will interrupted curtly. 'Sometimes we all have to do things we don't like to get what we want. Which brings me neatly back to the discussion your father and I were having when you knocked on the door.'

A tense glance passed between Will and Ardagh as they settled back into their chairs. Robin realised the two men had been arguing.

'We have evidence that Gisborne's allies are going to cheat to win the election,' Will explained.

'Do we know how?' Robin asked.

'The polling stations where people vote can't open unless they have the ballot boxes into which people post their votes,' Will began. 'I've had reports that the boxes delivered to many stations have been stolen. I also received a tip-off that staff haven't been assigned to work in some polling stations, so they won't be able to open. Or they'll be short-staffed and have massive queues that will put voters off.'

Robin sighed. 'Let me guess. It's happening on the housing estates and student areas where we think people are most likely to vote for us?'

'Of course,' Will agreed. 'And in a tight sheriff's election, even a few hundred votes could be the difference between winning and losing.'

Now Ardagh spoke to his son. 'Before you came in, I told Will that I'm determined to win this election honestly. But Will feels we should do a little cheating ourselves. Maybe pull a few fire alarms, or superglue the locks of voting stations in middle-class areas where people tend to vote for Gisborne.'

Robin smirked at the thought of mischief. 'Fight fire with fire. Why not?'

Ardagh tutted. 'Because it's *wrong*. Why stoop to their level?'

Will spoke crossly. 'If Gisborne becomes sheriff, thousands of people will suffer over the next four years. People ripped off, neighbourhoods flooded with drugs, folks thrown in jail because they went to hospital without proper documents or beaten by cops because they can't afford to pay a bribe. And if Marjorie sends in the army and turns Sherwood Forest into a war zone, it'll be a hundred times worse.'

Ardagh's expression suggested that Will's arguments had made an impression. Now Robin tried to speak seriously, which felt difficult while dressed in boxer briefs and Marion's daisy hoodie.

'Dad, the last time you stuck to your mighty principles, two crooked cops broke your legs and threw you in jail, while me and Little John escaped to the forest and almost got killed about twenty times. And the only reason Gisborne's thugs didn't finish you off in prison is that you were protected by a gang of misogynist, homophobic bikers who rob cars and sell drugs.'

Will smiled. 'We live in a morally complex world.'

'Stick to your principles *after* you've become Sheriff of Nottingham and you have some power,' Robin suggested.

Ardagh looked up at the ceiling and sighed deeply. 'It leaves a bitter taste in my mouth, but I suppose you're both right.'

Robin and Will smiled at each other.

'But nothing crazy,' Ardagh warned. 'I'll reluctantly accept a few sensible, measured steps to tilt the field of play back in my favour. But I don't want this cheating to get out of control.'

'Sensible and Measured are practically my middle names.' Robin grinned.

Will gave Robin a stern look. 'It's a weekday, and you're thirteen. You will be going back to Sherwood

Castle and spending election day at School Zone where you belong.'

'Quite,' Ardagh agreed, as Robin gawped. 'Last night's stunt was risky enough.'

'And protecting you and Marion in the cinema tied up a big chunk of my security team,' Will added. 'Today I need my best people on the street protecting our campaign staff.'

'Oh, come on!' Robin begged. 'It's the most important day ever, and I'm expected to sit on my arse in school, learning dumb stuff about the House of Tudor and drawing bowls of fruit?'

Ardagh made a rare attempt at humour. 'If you do a good fruit drawing, I promise I'll pin it on the fridge in the sheriff's office.'

This tickled Will, who struggled to keep a straight face as he spoke to the furious Robin. 'Emma is organising transport to take you and the other kids back to the castle for school. If you like, you can come back here this evening for the election results and the party if we win.'

Robin was steaming. If it hadn't been a total teenage cliché, he would have stormed out and told Will and his dad that he hated them. Instead, Robin scowled at the carpet as Ardagh checked the time and stood up to leave.

'Better get on the road,' Ardagh said. 'I have a radio interview in Nottingham at quarter to six, and Breakfast TV at seven.'

Robin was touched when his dad crossed the room and kissed him on the cheek for the first time in years.

'Stay safe and go to school,' Ardagh urged. 'I love you.'

'Love you too, Dad,' Robin said as Ardagh headed for the stairs. 'Now go out there and win!'

# 5. LITTLE BIT NAUGHTY

05:58

Robin's half-brother John had been dreading election day, with his mother Marjorie going for president, his father running for sheriff, and his girlfriend Clare being rival candidate Guy Gisborne's daughter.

His enormous seventeen-year-old body had a weird habit of waking up a few minutes before his weekday alarm, and as John stretched and scratched his armpit hair, 05:58 on the bedside clock confirmed that he'd done it again.

John assumed he was in his room at the fancy Barnsdale boarding school, just north of Sherwood Forest. But while he was definitely squeezed onto one of Barnsdale's single bunks, his wireless charging stand wasn't on the bedside table and the posters on the wall were wrong.

John sat bolt upright, making the duvet fly. 'Oh, balls!'

His girlfriend Clare was asleep in a padded office chair, her feet on her desk, while the Chemistry books and past exam papers they'd been going through the previous evening had slid to the floor.

Barnsdale had strict rules about spending the night in someone else's room. In one minute, alarms would go off in every room in Clare's boarding house and the corridor outside would be full of girls dashing to the washrooms to prep for school.

'Clare!' John yelped.

'Hey, you,' Clare said, smiling fondly, then stretching and giving a relaxed yawn. 'Is it after curfew? You'd better sneak back to your room before someone notices.'

'Forget curfew, it's *morning*,' John said. 'We slept all night.'

Clare guessed John was pranking her. But her phone said 05:59 when she checked and there was no denying day's first light creeping around the edges of the roller blind.

'We're dead if they find out you spent the night in my room!' Clare gasped as she stood up urgently, then rubbed her neck because it was stiff from sleeping in the chair. 'Why didn't you leave?'

'Why did you put the duvet over me?' John accused back.

'I thought you looked cute when you nodded off, so I covered you up. I didn't think you'd sleep the *whole* night.'

'When I sleep, I sleep,' John said, as he swung himself off the bed and looked around for his school blazer and size sixteen brogues.

'We'll get expelled,' said Clare desperately. 'They've been super strict since Lyn Tann got pregnant with triplets.'

'We didn't do *anything*,' John pointed out. 'We fell asleep studying.'

'But that's what they'll expect us to say,' Clare pointed out. 'No couple that gets caught is gonna say they spent the night shagging, are they?'

'Is anyone out in the corridor yet?' John asked.

Clare's 6am alarm beeped as she peeked into the corridor and saw five girls lined up down the end.

'They get up early to beat the bathroom queue,' Clare explained, then had an idea. 'Nobody will come in this room though. Can you sneak out when first lesson starts?'

John shook his head. 'But I won't be in my dorm, will I? The staff will look for me.'

'True.' Clare sighed. 'And everyone knows we're a couple, so this is the first place they'll look.'

'Even if they don't expel us, I guarantee they'll kick me off the rugby team,' John moaned.

Clare pulled up the roller blind. 'It's still pretty dark. You could go out of the window.'

'It's the second floor,' John said.

'But there's a bay window sticking out just below. Lower yourself down from the ledge onto that, then drop to the ground.'

'I'm heavy,' John protested. 'Not wild about heights either.'

A knock on the door made John dive for cover. It was followed by a high voice. 'You'd better be out of bed, Miss Gisborne! I'll not keep the breakfast room open if you're late again.'

'Yes, Miss Pledger,' Clare answered obediently before turning back to John and whispering nervously. 'Pledger hates me because of who my dad is. She'd love it if she caught you in here!'

'Window it is,' John said, resigning himself as he dragged Clare's bed away from the wall to get to the window. 'Promise you'll visit me in hospital if I break my legs.'

The tiles on the window ledge were crumbling, and the wooden sash squealed as John opened it.

'Ssssh!' Clare hissed.

There were chatty girls out in the hallway prepping for the school day now, so Clare's *ssssh* seemed excessive. But John hid his irritation as he leaned through the window frame, scraping the back of his neck on the bottom sash.

After a wary look into the gloom, John put one shoe on the window ledge. Unfortunately, the morning dew made the tiled ledge slippery and the leather soles of his handmade brogues had zero grip.

As John pulled his second leg through the window, his front shoe slipped. He couldn't fully regain his balance, but he was strong enough to stumble forward off the ledge, drop towards the flat zinc roof over the bay window and land with the grace of a falling brick.

The metal buckled under John's weight, and for an instant Clare thought he would go through the roof. After making a clumsy attempt to stay upright, John's forward momentum left him no choice but to make the next leap to the ground.

He landed on his feet, terrorising a squirrel as he demolished a section of a box hedge. As the branches snapped, John tipped forward onto the path, patterned with damp gravel that stuck to his school shirt and dug painfully into his palms as he threw out his arms to protect his face.

'Almighty God!' John gasped as he dragged himself out of the branches, then looked around urgently as he stood up.

Anyone near the bay window would have heard the metal clank and John's crash landing. But when John looked back, he realised he'd landed on the downstairs rec room, that only got used after school.

'Are you OK?' Clare asked from her window. She was shocked by the noise and the big dent in the metal roof, but Clare couldn't help smirking at her boyfriend, with his shirt torn at the shoulder, leaves in his hair and a twig sticking out of one ear.

'Don't laugh,' John growled. 'I almost died!'

Clare sensed his anger and fought off her smile. Then a light came on in the downstairs rec room and an adult marched straight for the bay window.

'I'll meet you after morning prayers with your bag and books,' Clare whispered as John ducked below hedge level and ran.

Clare backed into her room as the adult flung open the window below and yelled, 'I see you, young man!'

John knew his enormous size was enough to betray his identity, so he dropped onto his hands and crawled rapidly along the hedge until he reached the front of Clare's boarding house. As he stood and rapidly swept gravel off his trousers, a torch shone in his face.

'What are you doing down there?' Barnsdale's headmistress Ms Bao asked. 'And why did we track your phone to the girls' dormitory?'

The headmistress was flanked by a man and woman. The guy shining the torch was a chunky bloke in a Capital City police inspector's uniform. On Miss Bao's other side was a woman dressed like an office worker, but the gun and cuffs bulging under her blazer suggested she was also a cop.

John's brain was fixed on his escape and he almost blurted 'We fell asleep while we were studying.' But the presence of a police inspector signalled something much more serious.

'John Kovacevic?' the plain-clothes cop asked, stepping forward and flashing her police badge.

'Kovacevic's my mum's name. I use Hood, but most people call me Little John.'

'I'm Commander Thrush from the Capital City police. There are some matters we need to discuss, urgently.'

# 6. YA CAN'T HIDE

06:46

The White House got quieter after Ardagh left for his interviews and most campaign volunteers headed off in a fleet of hired buses.

Robin breakfasted on another bacon roll and a cheese omelette. When Marion woke up, the pair decided their best strategy was to lie low and hope the busy adults would forget about sending them to the castle for school.

They wound up in the huge house's deserted games room, passing time with ping-pong and a wall-mounted TV showing breakfast news. The presenter was getting mega dramatic about election day: 'It's less than fifteen minutes until polls open. Forty million adults will get to decide on our president for the next five years, and vote for hundreds of local officials, including mayors, sheriffs and judges.'

By 7.30am, Robin was sweaty, and fed up with Marion beating him at table tennis. Then her little brother Otto charged into the room, followed by Ten Man, as the eight-year-old yelled, 'I told you they were in here.'

Marion mouthed *you're dead, snitch*, and made a throat-cutting gesture at Otto as Ten Man spoke grumpily. 'What are you two idiots playing at? You've got ten minutes to gather your stuff and meet me out back.'

Robin decided to try his luck. 'Actually, my dad said I can stay here, seeing as it's election day.'

'No, he didn't,' Otto blurted. 'Will Scarlock said they've got to go to school with the rest of . . . Ow!'

Marion gave him a two-handed shove into the ping-pong table. As Otto rolled around like he'd been shot, Ten Man gave Robin a look of contempt. 'Do I look stupid?' he barked.

Otto looked pleadingly at Ten Man as he stumbled to his feet. 'Are you going to let her do that after I helped you find them?'

Ten Man shrugged. 'How old are you?'

'Eight,' Otto said.

Ten Man grunted. 'That's old enough to know nobody likes a tattletale.'

For a few seconds it looked like Otto would burst into tears, but he just said, 'I'm not bothered,' unconvincingly, then sprinted out.

Eight minutes later, Robin exited the rear of the White House into light drizzle. Ten Man had organised a convoy of three quad bikes. Two quads were attached to small trailers, each with eight kids squashed up on wooden bench seats.

'There's no room in those trailers,' Robin said as he neared Ten Man and a rebel volunteer called Beth.

Ten Man pointed out a pair of powerful dirt bikes nearby. 'You and Marion both ride. You'll take the bikes and cover the rear of the convoy. It's only 6k from here to Sherwood Castle, but every bandit in the forest knows that the rebel forces are stretched today, so we can't be too careful.'

'Gotcha, boss,' Robin said, feeling happier now he'd been upgraded from kid-being-driven-to-school to substitute security officer.

Marion looked happier too as she neared her bike and saw a compact machine gun hanging off the right handlebar.

'Know how to use that?' Ten Man asked.

'If I have to,' Marion said, checking to see if it was loaded, then taking a look down the gunsight.

'Robin, I assume you'll stick with your bow?' Ten Man asked. 'And you've both got your two-way radios charged?'

'I fell asleep before I put mine on charge last night, but there's enough battery for a ride to the castle,' Robin said.

'Let's roll out, people,' Ten Man shouted, as he signalled to Beth and another rebel who'd be driving the quads attached to trailers.

Little kids yelped excitedly as the three quad bike engines fired up. Robin gave himself a few seconds to put on his helmet and get a feel for the bike's controls, while Marion couldn't resist taking a selfie of herself, pulling her meanest expression as she straddled her bike with the machine gun slung around her neck.

But as Robin pulled away, a young woman in a raincoat sprinted out of the White House. He was forced to slam on the brakes as she thrust a little action camera on a stick in his face.

'Robin Hood,' the woman spluttered breathlessly. 'I'm Genna Delano, live-streaming for the *Courier* website. I'd like to know if you have an election day message for the wife and child of the prison officer you *brutally* murdered?'

Robin was stunned, but Marion hopped off her bike and violently shoved Genna backwards. As the little action camera hit the dirt, a rebel officer and a volunteer in a red *Vote Ardagh* T-shirt grabbed Genna under the arms.

'Leave Robin alone, you old bat,' Marion roared, as the journalist fought the pair trying to pull her away. 'Robin saved my life – and all the others that guard would have shot.'

'I am a journalist following a legitimate story,' Genna shouted, twisting and kicking as she got dragged away. 'Your hoodlums are assaulting me.'

Marion closed in to give Genna a kick, but Ten Man pulled her off and shouted furiously as two more security officers arrived on the scene.

'Escort this so-called journalist off the premises,' Ten Man boomed, as Marion noticed the action camera and pressed it into the muddy lawn with her boot heel. 'And someone tell Azeem to go back through surveillance recordings and find out how a *Courier* journalist got through our security perimeter.'

Marion looked at Robin as Genna was picked up and carried inside. 'You OK, mate?'

'Bit of a scare,' Robin admitted. 'I was about to open the throttle. Two seconds later I'd have run her over. And thanks for sticking up for me.'

'You'd do the same,' Marion said, then glanced over her shoulder. Emma Scarlock had rushed out to see what had happened, and Ten Man was yelling to nobody in particular about the security lapse being *beyond a joke*.

Ten Man calmed down when Emma assured him that she'd have a meeting with Security Chief Azeem, work out what had gone wrong and make sure it didn't happen again.

The kids waiting in the trailers had grown restless, and several young boys decided that they needed to pee and started running off into the trees.

Ten Man wasn't used to dealing with kids and his patience cracked. 'Any of you snot-nosed brats not back in the trailer in thirty seconds is getting a kick up the arse,' he shouted, glancing at his chunky diver's watch. 'I know you're all super keen to get to school on time!'

# 7. YM6

07:21

Ten Man kept his rifle loaded and ready as he led the school convoy over boggy cowpat-splattered fields, then into Sherwood Forest on a rutted path with puddles deep enough to make the kids in the trailers squeal as they blasted through.

Marion and Robin rode at the rear of the convoy, keeping an eye out for bandits – and enough distance not to get splashed by the quads.

The six-kilometre ride to Sherwood Castle took less than half an hour and the final stretch was up Sherwood Castle's grand front driveway. This arrow-straight road was once used by luxury cars travelling to the castle's five-star resort and hotel. Now, the rebels had dumped truckloads of rubble and set tank-traps made from welded scaffold poles, turning the driveway into a slalom that would stop cops or bandits storming in.

Marion loved to ride and couldn't resist speeding past the quad bikes and zipping close to the barricades, until she reached the castle resort's modern glass lobby.

As Robin pulled up behind, the pair jumped as a loud siren erupted from their yellow two-way radios. This only happened when someone hit the red emergency switch on top of their radio, giving them priority over all other signals on the network.

The voice that followed kept breaking up into metallic crunching sounds. Robin could barely hear, so he hurriedly took off his helmet.

'This is Teegan Edwards. I was on Battle Bus 5 and we got pulled by some badass cops who must be on Gisborne's payroll. I jumped out of the emergency exit window, but the rest are getting a tough time. One lady got slapped around for talking back. They've put cuffs on our driver, and they're threatening to impound our bus because they say the paperwork looks fake.'

Robin and Marion listened keenly to the reply from Rebel Control. 'This is headquarters. Edwards, what is your location?'

'We're on Route 9 heading west. Three cop cars came out of nowhere and made us pull into a layby. I don't know this area, but we're on the edge of the forest. I'm squatting down behind a shuttered King Corp petrol station and supermarket.'

Marion glanced knowingly at Robin. 'I know exactly where that is,' she whispered.

The rebel controller spoke over the radio. 'Edwards, I'm going to try and send help. I'll advise shortly.'

Thirty seconds passed before Rebel Control spoke again. 'We can get a camera drone there, which might make the cops think twice about behaving badly. Unfortunately, the nearest security officers are at least half an hour away.'

'Seriously?' Edwards shouted. 'Now the cops are making everyone line up against the side of the bus. They're stealing wallets and threatening them with stun guns.'

'Teegan, I need you to keep a safe distance, stay calm and let me know what's happening,' the controller said. 'I'm doing everything I can to get help to your location as soon as we can.'

Marion surprised Robin by grabbing her radio. Rebel radio signals were encrypted, but she still used her code name in case anyone was listening.

'This is YM6,' Marion began. 'I'm astride a bike right now. I know a path up to Route 9 that the Brigands use to bring in fuel. I can be there in ten to twelve minutes.'

There was a pause as the rebel controller looked up YM6's identity. Meanwhile, outside the castle, Ten Man and Beth were telling the little kids to get inside.

'Offer to assist appreciated, YM6,' the controller said. 'I'm checking with the boss to see if it's appropriate for you to be involved.'

'Appropriate!' Teegan yelled into his radio. 'We need help here right *now*!'

'Teegan, I'm doing all I can,' the controller said, still infuriatingly calm. 'Please await further information.'

Marion looked at Robin as Ten Man strode towards them.

'Authorisation, my arse,' Marion sneered to Robin as she put her helmet back on. 'Since when do we need permission to help people?'

'I'll come with you,' Robin said, cracking a smile as Marion restarted her bike.

'Fine, but you ride like an old lady. Try not to hold me up.'

Ten Man had his own radio, so he'd heard everything. 'Marion, I'll follow,' he began, but Marion cut him off.

'Not on a quad bike you won't. Brigands only made the path wide enough for two-wheelers.'

'There are bikes out back,' Ten Man said. 'I don't want you two haring off on your own.'

Marion tutted. 'Ten Man, by the time you walk halfway across the castle grounds and fiddle around finding a motorbike, I'll be at Route 9.'

'Will and Emma gave strict orders for me to keep you two safe,' Ten Man said.

'You'd better catch us up then,' Marion said before she blasted off. 'Route 24 will get you there in twenty minutes.'

Ten Man was close enough to yank Robin off his bike. He didn't, because although the two thirteen-year-olds were taking a big risk, Ten Man's gut told him they were doing the right thing.

The controller's voice came out of Ten Man's radio as Robin and Marion sped away. 'YM6, I've spoken to Azeem and she says to hold your position.'

Ten Man smirked as he spoke into his radio. 'Control, I think YM6 and AB19 have ignored your instructions. Let's give them all the back-up we can.'

# 8. MARJORIE'S GETTING NUKES

07:48

Barnsdale School had been around for five hundred years, and while no pupil had been caned in decades, John waited in an area outside the head's office that was still known as the whipping room.

He tried messaging Clare, but Barnsdale's extensive grounds were a graveyard for phone signals and the Wi-Fi in this building was for staff only. He sat chewing his thumbnail and tapping his feet for an hour. The only interruption came when a kitchen worker dropped off a red plastic tray with cold porridge and warm apple juice.

'Sorry to keep you waiting,' Commander Thrush said, her voice echoing down the vaulted stone hallway. She'd been given the key for a deputy head's office, where they could speak privately.

'I work for the National Police, assigned to the president's office for close protection duties,' Thrush began as John sat on a cracked leather sofa, facing Barnsdale's playing fields. 'I'm sorry I kept you waiting, but the entire force is on Level 1 alert for election day. I also had a chat with your headmistress about your overnight stay with Clare Gisborne—'

'We were just studying,' John interrupted. 'Revising always makes me fall asleep.'

Thrush smiled coyly. 'Luckily for you, your headmistress feels that a scandal involving the expulsion of the president's son and the daughter of a notorious gangster is the kind of publicity Barnsdale School could do without.'

'Awesome,' John said, relieved. 'Though I'm only the president's son if my mum wins.'

'True,' Thrush said. 'But polls give your mother a six-point poll lead and a 99.2 per cent probability of being president by this time tomorrow. You and I need to have a frank conversation, because your life won't be the same for as long as your mother remains in office.'

'You mean like, bodyguards and stuff?' John asked.

Thrush nodded. 'Though we prefer to call it close protection.'

'Can I still do normal stuff?'

'We don't have the power to stop you from doing anything, but we offer advice and hope you will cooperate for your own safety. As son of the president, you represent a security risk. We would strongly discourage you from engaging in certain activities, such as going to crowded concerts, where it would be difficult to protect you, or travelling to unfriendly countries.'

'How am I a security risk?' John asked. 'It's not like my mum's gonna be sharing state secrets with me.'

Thrush paused while she thought of a good explanation. 'A few minutes after your mother is sworn in as president, she'll be given a set of codes and a red key that enables her to use nuclear weapons. At any given time, this country has two nuclear submarines on patrol, each armed with ninety-two thermonuclear warheads capable of ending life as we know it on planet Earth.'

John knew that the president controlled nuclear weapons, but he'd never really thought about that person being his mum.

'Nukes!' he gasped, then shook his head slowly.

'Now, imagine you went on a school trip to Russia,' Thrush said. 'You get yourself kidnapped. In return for your release, the Russians demand that your mother gives them detailed information on our missile defence systems.'

'Does it happen?' John asked warily. 'Family of leaders getting kidnapped or blackmailed?'

'It's rare in developed countries,' Thrush said reassuringly. 'But only because close protection teams like mine work hard to keep you safe. You will be protected twenty-four hours a day by a team of officers, with three or four on duty at any given time.

'You can choose to have an officer in uniform by your side, but usually your protection squad will keep a discreet distance. We're not a chauffeur service, but it's usually simpler if you allow your protection team to drive you around. For instance, riding in a secure vehicle, rather than a crowded train.

'Our lives will be easier if you let us know what you're up to. It's also easier to protect you discreetly if you tell us your plans and we're able to scout locations before you get there. Does all that make sense?'

'I think so,' John said, nodding. 'But, like, what if I do something illegal when cops are protecting me? Not massive, like murder, but something loads of people do, like speeding, or buying booze with a fake ID?'

Thrush smiled. 'I wouldn't encourage you to break the law, but the duty of a close protection officer is to protect you. We will only intervene if you are in danger, or you put another person at risk of death or serious harm.'

John smirked. 'If I start a punch-up, will my protection officers finish it for me?'

Thrush had read enough background information to know that John was a gentle person and was making a joke. 'Let's not find out the answer to that question, eh? Now, if you are happy with what I've just said, I'd like to discuss your plans for the rest of today.'

'So, the protection starts now?' John asked.

'It was supposed to start this morning, but you weren't in your room when we knocked.'

John spent a few seconds remembering what he was up to. 'I've got morning prayers, free period, then the Chemistry exam me and Clare were studying for at ten. Lunch, more lessons, then rugby against Coventry Grammar School.'

'The match is here?' Thrush asked.

'Yeah, it's a home match. After rugby I've got special permission to leave school with my girlfriend, Clare. We're going to a People's Party event at the Grand Salon Hotel in Locksley to watch the election results. The sheriff's election result is expected around midnight. If Gisborne wins, I'll stay with Clare. If my dad wins, his people will collect me and take me over to the White House for their celebration.'

'That could be tricky,' Thrush said, as she tapped a note into her phone. 'Your father's campaign is backed by rebels and bikers. They won't appreciate the presence of plain-clothes police officers.'

'They definitely won't,' John said, half smiling, half squirming at the prospect. 'But I can put you in touch with Emma and Will, who are running my dad's campaign. Maybe you can come to an arrangement.'

'Hopefully,' Thrush said, as she tapped more notes into her phone. 'Though Will Scarlock is only a couple of places below your kid brother on the police Most Wanted list.'

John continued with his schedule. 'The result of the presidential election is due around one-thirty tomorrow morning. If my mum wins, I've got to be at the Presidential Palace in Capital City.

'There's some tradition where the new president appears on the palace balcony with their family at sunrise. But I have to try and sleep some time, because I've got to be back here for a Computer Science exam at noon.'

'A busy schedule,' Thrush noted.

John shrugged. 'My life's usually boring. Most days, I'll be here at school. On weekends I either hang out with Clare or at my mum's penthouse in Nottingham.'

'Do you visit your father?'

'We get along great, but he's been super busy with the sheriff's election. I've barely seen him since he got out of jail.'

'Thank you for being so cooperative,' said Thrush, smiling and standing up. 'I wish you luck in your Chemistry exam. I'll make plans based on your schedule. Then I'll catch up with you again at lunchtime and introduce you to Scott and some of the officers who'll be protecting you.'

'If I'm not eating lunch in the main hall, I might be with the guys in the weight room,' John said. 'Coach usually sets up a table with pasta and healthy stuff before a big match.'

'Don't worry,' Thrush said. 'It's my job to know where to find you.'

# 9. NEW KID IN THE FOREST

08:02

Robin had been riding motorbikes for a year and liked to think he'd become a decent rider. But Marion's biker father sat her on a mini-bike before she could walk, and her skills zipping along tight forest paths put him to shame.

'Come on, Grandma,' Marion teased, as she stopped for a third time to let Robin catch up.

Robin watched her disappear again, in a ballet of expert throttle control, fearlessly leaning into tight curves, and always seeming to know when to duck so a branch didn't smack her helmet.

They cut their noisy bike engines a few hundred metres from the Route 9 layby, then jogged until they found Teegan Edwards squatting at the rear of the gas station.

The handsome eighteen-year-old wore a denim jacket, a red *Vote Ardagh for Change* campaign shirt and an oversized metal badge that said *FIRST-TIME VOTER!*

'Wow, Robin and Marion!' Teegan gasped as the pair squelched through the mud towards him.

'What's the latest?' Robin asked.

'We can't hear our radios while riding,' Marion explained.

'Cops don't seem in any hurry to leave. Old guy mouthed off about his rights, so they dragged him in front of the bus and beat the daylights out of him.'

'How many cops?' Marion asked.

'Four cops, three cars,' Teegan answered. 'Two parked behind the bus, one up ahead on the road. There was a drone buzzing around too, but I've not heard it for a bit.'

Robin looked at a gutter pipe on the side of the abandoned gas station. 'I'll go up on the roof and see what's going on.'

Marion nodded in agreement. 'I'll circle around to the two cop cars at the back and give you cover. Teegan, how's your shooting?'

'Not bad,' Teegan said. 'I bought a bow and arrow last summer when everyone was wearing *Robin Hood Lives* T-shirts.'

Marion took her mini crossbow out of her pack and gave it to Teegan.

'Don't you need it?' he asked.

'I'm good,' Marion said, tapping her machine gun.

While Marion and Teegan crept out to the two cop cars behind the bus, Robin pulled himself up the gutter pipe to the flat canopy over the petrol station forecourt.

His boots squelched through moss and composted leaves as he made a crouching run. Then he peered down from the roadside edge to take in the scene.

Battle Bus 5 was a thirty-eight-seater that had seen better days. Robin was appalled when he saw the old guy Teegan mentioned, slumped in front of the bus, bloody from his beating.

The driver had been cuffed and forced to lie face down in the road, while twenty campaign workers had been made to line up alongside the bus and empty everything from their pockets. They now stood with their palms against the side of the bus and the contents of their pockets scattered around their feet.

Robin noticed one cop inside the coach searching bags and holding at least three laptops. Another stood on the road, near the car, looking twitchy, while the last two worked down the line of passengers, inspecting belongings on the ground and taking anything of value.

A young cop with a bushy red beard seemed to be in love with his own voice as he searched.

'Look here!' he taunted, as he picked a wallet off the ground and pocketed sixty bucks. 'Is that phone the new G25? How does anyone voting for that monkey Ardagh have enough money for a G25? Are you a thief, son? I'm gonna need you to spread your legs a little wider.'

Robin pulled his bow out of his pack and mentally plotted the best way to take out four cops. The three in the open would be easy, but the gently tinted bus windows caught the early morning light, making the officer inside impossible to target.

'Now, you slimy communist gimp, let me see what's in that shirt pocket,' the bearded cop demanded, as he moved on to his next victim. 'Spread your legs, wider . . . wider!'

Robin watched as the activist leaning against the bus spread his legs until it looked like his jeans would rip.

'Wider,' the cop demanded. 'Are you deaf as well as stupid?'

'It's killing my back,' the guy being searched said, straining with pain.

'OK, lift your right leg,' the officer snarled. 'Now lift your left leg.'

The guy put his right leg down, then lifted his left. The red bearded cop thumped him between the shoulder blades with his baton.

'I said lift your left leg,' the officer spat. 'Did I say put your right leg down?'

'How can I raise both legs?'

'Like this,' the cop said, then hooked his boot around the man's ankle and swept it away.

The activist yelled in pain as he slid down the side of the bus, making Robin wince when his knees hit the road.

'Rebel scum gets what it deserves,' the cop shouted.

Robin looked away, first at the other cop doing searches, who was stamping on a sobbing woman's phone, then at the cop inside the bus, as he stepped out.

Now Robin could take them all out: notch five arrows, shoot the twitchy cop standing by his car first, aim slightly left and shoot the female officer who'd just stepped off the bus, then left and left again to take out the pair doing searches. It would be over in eight seconds, with a spare arrow just in case . . .

They were easy shots at this distance, and even if the cops wore stab-proof vests, they were designed to stop a thrusting knife, not an arrow doing a hundred kilometres per hour. But Robin hesitated as he grabbed five arrows from his pack.

Marion's voice came over Robin's radio. 'I'm in position with Teegan. Eyes on two cop cars and the back of the bus. How about you?'

Robin suddenly felt queasy. 'I . . . Yeah . . . The sun is low. Right in my eyes so it's hard to shoot. Ten Man should be here soon. Maybe we should wait.'

As Robin said this, the female cop who'd stepped off the bus threw her haul of stolen tablets, laptops and designer sunglasses onto the passenger seat of the front car. On the way back to the bus, she opened her pepper spray and blasted the old guy who'd taken a beating.

'How are those civil rights of yours now?' the cop taunted, before erupting in laughter.

Marion's voice came back over the radio. 'If you can't shoot, I'm gonna blast the cop cars. Hopefully it'll distract the cops long enough for people to run off.'

Robin's chest and arms were tense, and when he tried to breathe it felt like a big, gloved hand was clamped over his mouth. He'd managed to notch the arrows, but he kept seeing the picture on the *Courier* website with the dead prison guard's wife and son.

*I'm gonna puke,* he thought.

Robin's anxious train of thought was broken by a massive blast of gunfire, shattering glass and tearing metal as Marion unleashed her machine gun on the two cop cars behind the bus.

The twitchy cop who'd stayed by the police car in front of the bus dived for cover, then shouted, 'I told you! We're too close to the forest to stick around this long.'

'Let's go,' the female officer agreed.

Two cops joined the twitchy officer in a mad scramble towards the surviving police car. But the mouthy, bearded officer couldn't resist a final greedy swoop to steal a wallet.

'Oh, no you don't,' Robin snarled as he took aim.

As Marion stepped into the road and blasted more holes in police cars, Robin shot an arrow perfectly through the back of the thieving cop's hand.

The three cops who'd reached the surviving car made zero effort to save their colleague. As they squealed off in a cloud of tyre smoke, activists who'd been tormented and humiliated by the bearded officer launched at him with spit and kicks.

Robin made a dramatic leap from the garage roof.

'Break it up,' he shouted as he charged into the scrum. 'Imagine the newspaper headlines: *Ardagh campaigners batter innocent police officer.*'

'But he's scum,' a woman shouted, spitting again. 'Our driver's got a broken arm. Ernest took an almighty beating, and those pigs drove off with thousands in cash and tech.'

But most campaigners saw Robin's logic. As they backed away, Robin saw the officer's bloody clenched fist, with the last wallet he'd tried to steal pinned to it by his arrow. Somehow, it felt very right and very wrong at the same time.

'Everyone OK?' Marion asked, looking like an undersized action movie hero as she strode away from the wrecked police cars with the machine gun around her neck. Then she looked up at the sky and gave Robin a baffled look. 'I'm surprised you couldn't shoot. The sun doesn't seem that bright.'

'Maybe shooting four cops wasn't the best strategy on election day,' Robin said. 'Scaring them off worked a treat.'

But this wasn't the whole truth. While Marion's tactic to scare the cops away had worked brilliantly, Robin hadn't been thinking about bad press or using a different strategy when he'd been up on the roof. He hadn't been able to shoot at the cops who'd been ripping people off and had horribly beaten an old man.

'I chickened out,' Robin muttered to himself as Marion jogged off to help a woman in tears.

*My head's all messed up.*

*I don't think I can do this any more . . .*

# 10. EVERYBODY'S STUFFING

08:26

Ten Man and a bunch of rebels who'd been at the castle arrived minutes after the three cops fled. The broken-armed bus driver and the old guy who'd been beaten were cleaned up and given emergency treatment, before they were loaded on the back of quad bikes for a bumpy ride to Dr Gladys' clinic at Sherwood Castle.

Nobody wanted to stick around in case the cops came back with reinforcements. They left the officer with the arrow through his hand at the side of the road, while Teegan and the rest of the campaigners hurriedly boarded Battle Bus 5. It set off with a substitute driver and two armed security officers for protection.

Robin and Marion jogged into the forest to collect their bikes, and quickly caught up with the battle bus. With several injured passengers, everyone in shock and having had their phones and money stolen, Ten Man decided they should return to the White House.

There were nerves when a Locksley police drone tailed the bus, but it peeled off after a few minutes and there were no more dramas on the twenty-five-minute drive.

Robin and Marion expected campaign HQ to be calm, like when they'd left. But when the pair dumped their muddy crash helmets in the hallway, Maud Newman's giant house was in chaos.

Will Scarlock yelled down from the top of the stairs. Azeem was screaming something about Photoshop. Emma led a line of campaign volunteers unloading boxes of printer paper from a van, while Marion's mum Indio and another bunch of volunteers were getting ready to go out, shouting, 'We need the cash now! Who has keys to the safe?'

Robin almost got knocked flying by Emma and Will's youngest son, nineteen-year-old Neo.

'Robin,' Neo Scarlock gasped as he steadied himself. 'You do computers, right? Can you do Photoshop?'

'I'm more into hacking than design,' Robin said. 'But Marion did a wicked Photoshop project at School Zone.'

'Really?' Neo said, turning to Marion and pointing in the direction of the printing room. 'Desai, who designed all our posters and campaign brochures, went up north on a campaign bus. I need you to go in the print room and offer your Photoshop skills to Joyce.'

'Who's Joyce?' Marion asked. 'Can I at least pee first?'

'Pee quickly!' Neo urged. 'Joyce is the one with purple dreadlocks.'

As Marion charged to the toilet, Robin decided to chase Neo towards the front door. 'Everyone's gone mental. What's going on?'

Neo stopped and took a big impatient breath. 'We've had a dozen tip-offs from supporters working in polling stations. As well as stopping deliveries of ballot boxes and short-staffing polling centres, it seems Gisborne has printed up tens of thousands of fake voting papers. His people have bribed or threatened staff in polling centres and they are *literally* going into polling stations and stuffing thousands of fake votes into ballot boxes.'

'We're screwed,' Robin said, then understood the whole crazy thing with paper, printers and Photoshop. 'But we're trying to make our own fake votes?'

Neo nodded. 'We need someone good with Photoshop to create exact copies of sixty different ballot papers.'

'Aren't they all the same?'

'If only,' Neo said. 'But as well as sheriff and president, there are votes for local council members. So there are different ballot papers in each area. My dad has sent people out with cash to buy every sheet of paper and laser printer they can lay hands on. We're also trying to locate a cutting machine that can trim printed A4 pages down to the right size.'

'Does my dad know we're doing this?'

Neo shook his head. 'Ardagh's busy doing interviews until midday. Will made the decision to go ahead without him.'

'My dad might take the moral high ground and say no to cheating,' Robin pointed out. 'And it sounds like Gisborne has been planning this for weeks. Even if we design and print loads of ballot papers, how do we get them from here to polling stations?'

Neo pointed at the ceiling, as Marion ran downstairs from the toilet and zipped across the hallway towards the print room. 'My brother Sam is running a meeting upstairs, with a bunch of people trying to figure out how we get fake votes into ballot boxes.'

Robin cracked a big smile, and Neo realised what he was thinking.

'That kinda sounds like a meeting Robin Hood should be involved in,' Neo said.

'I'm there already!' Robin said excitedly as he dodged a hand cart loaded with two boxed laser printers and bolted for the stairs.

# 11. BACK IN THE GAME

13:02

Ardagh's campaign was short of people. While the grown-ups had a million things to think about, Robin had wormed his way back into the action. He now sat in the back of a compact van, wearing a fur trapper's hat that hid most of his face.

Ísbjörg and twenty-year-old Sam Scarlock rode up front, while the rest of the van's cargo area contained eighteen thousand ballot papers that had been designed, printed, chopped, votes filled in with pencil, then folded in half and stuffed into white bin liners.

The signal on Robin's phone was erratic, but as the van moved towards Locksley, he managed to stream the one o'clock news headlines. He got a surprise when the news cut to his dad, dressed in his election-day suit, walking into a polling station as Guy Gisborne came out.

'While most of today's political activities have been carefully scripted,' the newsreader read stiffly, 'there was a tense and unplanned meeting when rival sheriff candidates Ardagh Hood and Guy Gisborne crossed paths while casting their votes at a Locksley polling station.'

Robin felt weird watching his dad and his arch enemy, both on their best behaviour, as they shook hands, smiled for the cameras and insincerely wished each other well. Gisborne even held a baby before ducking into his limo.

'Final polls showed Gisborne and Hood neck and neck in the Nottingham sheriff's race. But there have been reports of difficulties at polling stations across Nottinghamshire this morning, with some failing to open, lengthy queues, and reports of hooligans hurling beer cans and jars of pasta sauce at students queuing to vote at Beeston Arts College.'

The satnav announced they'd arrived. Robin zipped his phone into his hoodie pocket as the little van drove slowly past about sixty people queuing in front of an infant school that was being used as a polling station.

Sam turned into a side street, parked the van alongside the school's wire fence and walked around the back to let Robin out.

'Keep your hat on and your face low,' Sam warned as he grabbed four bags stuffed with fake votes. 'Try not to get recognised.'

After sitting in the windowless cargo area, the sun dazzled Robin as he stepped out. Ísbjörg led the way through a little side gate used for taking out the school's wheelie bins.

'Unlocked, as promised,' she said as the gate clanked.

The trio moved swiftly along a paved path to a door propped open with a mop and bucket. Robin got a noseful of pine disinfectant as he entered the school's kitchen, then a fright as a huge middle-aged woman bobbed up from behind a shiny metal catering bench.

'Bloody 'ell, you're Robin 'ood!' the woman said in a heavy northern accent. 'My grandson won't believe this!'

Sam spoke urgently. 'Where are Gisborne's men?'

'Voting happens in the school hall at the end of the main hallway,' the woman explained, as she pointed. 'When polling opened, these two leather jacket goons showed up. Scared the wits out of Julie and Marion, who are running the polling station.

'They made nasty threats, saying they knew where the women lived and what Gisborne would do to their children if they didn't let them sit in the staffroom with the ballot boxes.

'Blokes didn't realise I were back here in my kitchen. I've run dinners at this school for thirty year. And I told headmaster I'd come in today to unlock building for polling day. I stayed on for a bit, because I like my kitchen spotless and certain jobs are easier when no bugger's around.

'Soon as I heard those blokes putting frighteners on two young women, I called my Kelly. She's at uni in town and her boyfriend's been working on Ardagh's campaign.'

'Your tip-off was really important,' Sam told the meal supervisor. 'When my dad, Will, started looking into it, we found evidence that this has happened at polling stations all over Locksley, and further afield.'

'Are Gisborne's men in the staffroom now?' Ísbjörg asked.

The meal supervisor nodded. 'Every couple of hours, Julie or Marion takes a full ballot box out of the hall to the staffroom. Boxes are supposed to stay sealed until they're collected and taken to Locksley town hall after polling closes at nine-thirty, but them two nasty pieces of work have been in there all day. I haven't dared step out of my kitchen, but I assume they're fishing out all votes for Ardagh.'

'Where's the staffroom?' Sam asked.

'Out to hallway, then second door on right.'

'How many exits does it have?'

'Just one.'

'No time to waste,' Sam told Robin and Ísbjörg, then turned back to the meal supervisor. 'It's probably best if you don't hang around, in case something goes wrong.'

'Right-o,' she said. 'Just let me put on coat and get waffles from freezer. They need to defrost for breakfast club in morning.'

As the meal supervisor headed out, past the line of wheelie bins, Robin took the bow out of his backpack and notched three arrows.

Ísbjörg led a furtive jog down the infant school's central corridor, glimpsing queuing voters through the frosted glass door at the far end. As she pulled out a pistol with a silencer, Sam booted the staffroom door open and Robin burst in. Two men looked up from their phones in shock.

'I'm Hood,' Robin announced boldly as he stepped in, aiming his bow. 'Drop phones and put hands on heads. Piss me off and I'll shoot you through the eyeball.'

*Could I?* Robin wondered.

The two men had the same bulky frame, green eyes and flat nose. But they were decades apart in age, so Robin guessed father and son.

There were six rectangular ballot boxes stacked against the back wall, and the pair had made no attempt to hide what they'd been up to. The staffroom bin overflowed with ballot papers they'd stripped out of the boxes, while a stack of fake voting papers lay on a coffee table, along with the pencils they'd been using to cast hundreds of votes for their boss.

As Robin kept his bow aimed at the thugs, Sam opened a metal ballot box and looked at some of the votes.

'Every vote in here is for Gisborne,' he said, holding up a few papers. 'They're not even being subtle about it.'

'My youngest daughter is a terrific fan of yours, actually,' the daddy thug told Robin, trying to win favour as he sat with his hands on his head. 'You know what teenage girls are like. Eats vegan, says I should vote

Ardagh. And she loved that show where you sprayed paint all over Guy Gisborne's house.'

'*Truth to Power with Darrell Snubs*,' the younger thug said, smiling warily. 'My dad's whole crew cracked up when we watched it. Not around Gisborne, obviously. He'd have had our thumbs lopped off.'

The last thing Robin wanted was to be charmed by guys he might have to shoot.

'Shut your gobs,' Robin snapped, as a slight wobble of his bow betrayed the uncertain shudder in his arms.

# 12. DADDY THUG & BABY THUG

13:17

Once Sam had all six ballot boxes open, he scooped the votes for Gisborne into a black rubbish bag. Ísbjörg replaced them with their stack of pre-filled votes for Ardagh, plus some from the kitchen bin.

'Leave a few ballots for Gisborne in each box,' Sam said. 'Then the fraud isn't completely obvious.'

'Ten to fifteen per cent,' Ísbjörg agreed, as she sprinkled the first ballot box with a few votes for Gisborne, then churned the papers around before snapping the metal lid back on.

When all six boxes had been resealed, Sam turned his attention to the two thugs.

'I can't let you lads walk out and tell your boss what happened,' Sam explained as he unzipped his backpack and pulled out plastic gags and a bundle of heavy-duty cable ties. 'They'll find you when school opens in the morning.'

'No way!' the younger thug blurted, rearing out of his seat.

'Still!' Robin ordered, stepping forward.

'I have an enlarged prostate!' the daddy thug added. 'I'll wet myself.'

Robin smirked as Ísbjörg raised her silenced pistol and spoke dryly. 'We can tie you up until the kiddies arrive for school tomorrow, or shoot you through the head. It's your choice.'

'Would your boss give *us* that choice?' Sam added harshly.

'We just work for Gisborne,' the daddy thug said. 'No jobs around. Gotta feed my kids.'

Sam tutted contemptuously as he bound the younger thug's tattooed wrists with thick cable ties.

'Everyone has a choice not to be evil,' Sam growled as he stretched the elastic strap attached to a plastic mouth gag. 'Open wide.'

Once father and son had wrists and ankles bound and gags stuffed in mouths, Robin put his bow down and helped Sam drag the pair to a classroom across the hall. It had little-kid-sized furniture and a display with ABC charts and pictures of forest creatures.

'Teacher might get a shock when she arrives in the morning,' Robin noted, as Sam used more cable ties to attach the men to a heating pipe running along the back wall.

A key fob dropped out of daddy thug's leather jacket.

'And what have we here?' Sam asked.

'Tesla,' Robin purred, as Sam jangled the fob off his index finger. 'Nice wheels for a guy who says he's just working to feed his kids . . .'

Sam put on his best baby voice. 'Robin, do you think we should confiscate the vehicle to teach the naughty man a lesson?'

Robin laughed as daddy thug kicked a school chair and growled into his gag.

'I believe you should,' Robin said, copying Sam's baby voice. 'Especially as the naughty man is trying to call you a very rude name!'

'Later, gents,' Sam said, giving father and son a cheeky salute, then backing out of the classroom behind Robin.

'Why are you two smirking?' Ísbjörg asked grumpily as she dragged two black bags filled with Gisborne votes down the hallway towards the kitchen.

'Tesla, Tesla!' Sam sang, jangling the fob again.

'Teslas have trackers and need software updates,' Robin pointed out as they walked. 'That car's a brick once it's reported stolen. But if you drive it away and give the Brigands the key, they'd pay you a couple of thousand and strip it for parts.'

'Carry one of these,' Ísbjörg said, then tutted as she thrust a bag of Gisborne votes at Sam. 'There isn't time to mess around with cars. We have a list of polling stations to visit.'

'I know,' Sam said defensively, as they crossed through the school kitchen and out into daylight. 'I'm just dreaming of a life where I can afford new boots and jeans that haven't been patched by my mum.'

Robin was still laughing. 'Seriously, Ísbjörg. The older guy's face was a picture when Sam took his car key.'

'But you're right,' Sam told Ísbjörg sadly as he lifted the lid of a stinking food waste bin and dropped the Tesla fob in the sticky gunk at the bottom. 'Where to next?'

Ísbjörg was stepping through the school's side gate, but before she could answer Sam, all three got the emergency nee-naw blast from their walkie-talkies.

'This is Control,' the tinny voice began, as Robin pulled out his radio and upped the volume. 'I'm asking everyone on the street to be on extra high alert. It's just come on the radio that a bomb has gone off outside a north Locksley polling station. They don't think anyone was killed, but there are reports of injuries and the damaged polling station has been forced to close. I'll keep you up to date, but please, everyone, keep safe.'

Robin and Ísbjörg gawped in shock as Sam unlocked the van.

'Gisborne,' Sam snarled. 'Is there anything that man won't stoop to?'

As Sam opened the van's rear doors and flung in the bag of votes, Robin looked thoughtfully at the sky and Ísbjörg kicked the van.

'This election could turn *really* nasty,' Robin said.

'Shall we carry on, or wait until Control gives us more information about the bomb?' Ísbjörg asked.

Robin had zero doubts. 'I'd sooner risk getting blown up than let Gisborne become sheriff without putting up a fight.'

'I agree with the little brat,' Sam said.

'Hey!' Robin protested.

Ísbjörg smiled ruefully and pointed her finger back towards the main road. 'Next stop is Grange Mount community centre. Two kilometres thataway.'

# 13. I PREDICT A RIOT

14:10

Grange Mount community centre turned out to be a doddle. Gisborne's crew had visited a few hours earlier, dropping off five ballot boxes stuffed with fake votes and threatening to strangle the elderly couple staffing the polling station if they told anyone.

The election official bravely explained that he was eighty-two and that 'Iris and I have run every election at this polling station for fifty years and we're not gonna be bullied by that little fart, Guy Gisborne.'

It took Robin, Sam and Ísbjörg ten minutes to empty five metal boxes and swap Gisborne votes for Ardagh votes. The old guy even brought out tea and chocolate biscuits while they worked.

The third stop on Ísbjörg's list was a village polling station, eight kilometres south.

'Make sure we use the right ballot papers for this area,' Sam told Robin, as he drove through one of Locksley's many deserted streets. 'Can you dig them out, ready for when we arrive?'

'Sure,' Robin agreed, as his phone lit up his face in the gloomy rear compartment. 'Just checking the latest on the bombing.'

Robin looked at social media first. Eyewitnesses had posted photos of a polling station tent set up in the concourse of an outdoor shopping mall. The tent had been turned to a tangle of metal by the blast and a plastic dustbin had melted, but the most damage was to the windows of nearby shops.

'Doesn't look like a huge blast,' Robin told Sam and Ísbjörg as he studied the pictures. 'Police say it was just minor injuries. But the weird thing is, the mall where it happened looks well posh. The trashed shops are an organic supermarket, a Pilates studio and a Muffin Shack.'

'What area exactly?' Ísbjörg asked.

Robin checked the mall's location in his maps app. 'North-west Locksley. Close to the posh housing estates at Queen's View, where my mate Alan used to live.'

'It can't be!' Sam gasped. 'Why would Gisborne bomb a polling station in a wealthy area, where people are most likely to vote for him?'

'False flag operation?' Ísbjörg suggested. 'Gisborne plants a bomb in the nicest part of town, then gets corrupt Locksley cops to blame it on rebels?'

'I wouldn't put that past him,' Robin agreed.

'But rebels have no history of bomb-making,' Sam said. 'And if Gisborne was going to bomb something to try to make the rebels look bad and help him win the election, why do it halfway through election day?'

Robin thought for a second before nodding. 'Loads of people cast their votes before it happened,' he agreed.

'But who'd do that apart from Gisborne?' Ísbjörg asked.

Robin scrolled some more posts on his phone. 'It makes no sense. At least nobody got killed.'

Sam's phone rang. It was his mum, Emma Scarlock, but since he was driving, he passed the device to Ísbjörg in the passenger seat. Robin scooted up to the seats to listen and caught most of the conversation.

Emma told them that the woman at the polling station they were heading towards had got cold feet about letting them in. Apparently two guys were sitting outside in a car and she was pretty sure they worked for Gisborne.

'What's the new plan?' Ísbjörg asked.

Emma told them to drive back into town and liaise with a larger van where they could replenish their supply of fake voting papers before heading to another community centre. She added that there were now seven rebel teams taking fake votes to polling stations in Locksley and the surrounding areas.

The rebels' target was to get inside a hundred polling stations before polls closed at 9.30pm. So far, none of the teams had hit trouble, but it was only a matter of time before someone tipped off Gisborne's people and things got harder.

As Ísbjörg ended the call and gave Sam directions for their liaison, Robin picked up a burst of new social media notifications on his phone.

'You guys won't believe the latest,' Robin blurted as he read. 'The Pilates studio that got all its windows blown out is owned by Guy Gisborne's *wife*. And someone uploaded CCTV of two bikers dumping a package in a dustbin about ten minutes before it exploded.'

'Seriously?' Sam said.

'Were the bikers Brigands?' Ísbjörg asked.

'Looks like it,' Robin said. 'Their faces were covered, but they wore jackets with gang insignia on the back. No attempt to hide who they were.'

'Do Brigands even care about politics?' Ísbjörg said.

'I doubt it,' Robin said thoughtfully. 'But the Brigands bike gang and Gisborne's crew have been at each other's throats for ages. Last year, Brigands nicked over a million bucks' worth of cars from Gisborne's luxury car dealership. Gisborne got revenge by using his police connections to close down biker bars and target the chop shops and scrapyards where Brigands break up stolen cars.'

'Everyone assumes the polling station tent was the target,' Sam said. 'But maybe it was Gisborne's wife's studio.'

'But why on election day?' Ísbjörg asked.

Robin thought about this for a few moments as Sam took the van up a ramp and onto a deserted six-lane highway.

'Two reasons I can think of,' Robin began. 'First, Brigands and the other bike gangs don't want Gisborne becoming sheriff because it gives him more power and he'll use it to make his enemies' lives hell. Second, if you want to start a fight with Gisborne on his home turf, why not do it today when his muscle is spread all over the county trying to steal an election?'

Sam didn't seem convinced. 'But one small bomb isn't much.'

Robin had already considered this and was scanning his phone, searching for recent information with the keywords *Brigands* or *bikers*. There was nothing on the mainstream news websites, but when he checked social media he got dozens of results.

'Looks like it's kicking off everywhere,' Robin said, stunned, as he read through the search results. 'Besides the bomb, there's a video of bikers smashing up a dental clinic and an Italian restaurant that Gisborne owns. Two Gisborne car dealerships have been raided. A biker threw petrol bombs into Gisborne's casino, and there's other stuff too.'

'How can we not have heard about this?' Sam asked disbelievingly.

Robin shrugged. 'When mainstream media is busy covering an election, I guess a few punch-ups and robberies in Locksley can slip under the radar.'

'But Brigand attacks won't have gone under Gisborne's radar,' Sam said warily. 'He'll reorganise his people and send them after the bikers.'

'Which means less thugs free to go after us,' Ísbjörg noted optimistically.

'It's already tense out there with the election,' said Robin. 'If it's also kicking off with Gisborne and the Brigands, I can easily see this turning into another Locksley riot.'

# 14. LOCKER ROOM LADS

14:55

Barnsdale School's grounds were spread over a thousand acres of South Yorkshire countryside, but the place felt tiny when there was gossip flying around.

And no gossip was hotter than a first team rugby player leaping out of his girlfriend's bedroom window, being caught by the headmistress, then mysteriously only getting a telling-off for an offence that normally meant being suspended.

Little John felt good after rugby. Muddy legs, a grazed elbow, and the mix of excitement and exhaustion that comes after a hard game, won with a breakaway try minutes from the end.

John's knee had been strapped before the game, and the school's physio team wanted to check the injury afterwards. He waited five minutes in Barnsdale's fancy sports medicine suite while staff dealt with a player who'd torn a shoulder muscle.

After a few gentle stretches and some movement tests, the assistant physio announced that John's knee looked good. Less good was being the last player to arrive in the changing room; he caught everyone's attention.

After a good win, the team always ran into the showers in their muddy kit and jumped around doing manly hugs, back slaps and chest bumps hard enough to splat weaker teammates against the tiles.

'Look, it's shagger!' someone shouted when they saw John through the steam.

'Mr Untouchable,' Henry the team captain teased as he towelled off. 'When Mummy's about to become president, you're allowed to spend all night getting it on with the Gisborne!'

'Get stuffed, Henry,' John grumbled as he peeled his muddy shirt and tight-fitting base layer over his head.

John didn't really mind, because in the world of seventeen-year-old boys there are worse things to be teased about than your mates thinking you spent the night having sex with your girlfriend.

Most of the other guys were starting to dress, but the shower floor was a mass of abandoned kit and puddled brown water. As John raised one leg to take off a sock, a pair of soggy shorts slapped him in the back.

John instantly balled his sock and whipped it at Henry. The team captain ducked and John's sock hit the wall, leaving a muddy splat. But the rest of the team liked the idea and John got pelted with kit from all directions.

'I'll kick all your asses!' John growled, shielding his face with his arms, but smiling because it was all in fun.

'I'm surprised you played well,' Henry taunted. 'You can't have had much sleep last night.'

'I fell asleep studying,' John said, ready to drop his shorts but self-conscious because everyone was looking his way.

'Studying Clare Gisborne's naughty bits!' Henry said, as another team shirt flew through the air.

John realised his teammates would keep teasing him unless he took control, and he remembered a prison movie where someone said the best way to establish dominance is to go after the leader.

Henry Devereux was the star of the Barnsdale team, and had a real chance of turning professional. He was muscular, 188 cm tall, and had floppy blond hair that had half the girls and quite a few of the boys lusting after him.

John Hood was the only person at Barnsdale big and fast enough to bolt across a slippery floor, lock his arms around Henry's waist and flip him over his left shoulder.

'Meathead!' Henry roared. 'Put me down.'

A huge gasp whooshed around the changing room, followed by joyous anticipation as the team realised that Henry wasn't going to wriggle out of Little John's colossal arms.

'Head's going down the toilet, pretty boy,' John said.

Everyone backed up, giving John a clear path towards the changing room's appallingly filthy toilet cubicles.

A cheering, half-dressed crowd followed the action, chanting, 'Bog wash! Bog wash! Bog wash!'

John was a gentle soul, so nobody quite believed he'd dunk his team captain in the toilet. But John carried Henry into the graffiti- and mud-splattered cubicle and let him get a lungful of stink as his floppy hair dangled over the bowl.

'What the blazes is going on here?' head coach Runcorn shouted, as the bald-headed ex-rugby player crashed through the door at the far end of the room.

Runcorn was big, loud and scary, so most of the team scarpered back to the changing benches. John flipped Henry back the right way up and planted him on the toilet seat.

'What are you two doing back there?' the coach roared as he approached.

'Number two, sir,' Henry said, smiling cheekily up from the toilet. 'Privacy, please!'

The coach didn't see the funny side as he stepped back to the main changing area and roared at his team. 'I'm going for afternoon tea in the staffroom. When I get back in half an hour, this changing room had better be spotless and you lot long gone. If it's not up to scratch, I'll have the lot of you up at five tomorrow doing bronco busters until you hurl! Do you hear me?'

'Yes, Coach,' the team roared.

John hoped that the coach had finished, but he stepped in front of John and looked up at him. 'And you'd better get a move on, Little John. There's a presidential limousine outside, with your squeeze waiting patiently in the back.'

As the coach headed back to his office, the half-dressed lads poured out to take a look. Including John, in dripping wet team shorts and a single sock.

There were enough seriously rich kids at Barnsdale that getting dropped off in a helicopter was no big deal. But the school had never been graced with one of the country's huge black presidential limousines, custom-built to withstand terrorist bombs, armour-piercing bullets and poison gas.

Clare gave John a smile and a thumbs up from behind fifteen centimetres of bulletproof glass.

'That's some proper showing off,' a prop forward called Olu joked.

One teammate added, 'You'll jump the queue at any nightclub if you roll up in that!'

John shivered and cringed with embarrassment as a stocky plain-clothes policeman walked around the front of the limousine.

'I'm Sergeant Scott,' the man said. 'I'm in charge of your protection squad for the next twelve hours. Is everything OK? You look a little concerned.'

John gawped and dripped as his teammates listened. 'That thing is huge!' he finally blurted.

'Commander Thrush carried out a risk assessment,' Scott explained. 'There have been reports of electoral fraud and gang violence in Locksley today. Given the high chance that things could turn worse, it seemed sensible to use an armoured limousine from the presidential fleet.'

'Right,' John said, as he gave Clare a little wave back. 'I . . . er . . . I'd better shower and put my suit on.'

# 15. AFTERNOON PHISHING

16:55

The sun was starting to drop. Robin's stomach growled as he sat in the back of the van. They were parked outside Thunderbird Chicken, with Ísbjörg sitting up front reading emailed instructions for their next job, while Sam was in the restaurant picking up their order.

'I can't believe that nutty woman at the last polling station,' Robin said. 'First she tries to take out Sam with a stun stick, then we tie her up and she has the cheek to ask me to sign an autograph.'

'Uh-huh,' Ísbjörg said, more interested in her email.

'But I've got a good feeling,' Robin said. 'So many of the people we've met hate Gisborne.'

'But they're also terrified of him,' Ísbjörg said, less optimistically. 'There are over four hundred polling stations across the county and we're already running out of people brave enough to let us inside. Plus, I keep seeing smoke.'

'There's online video of shops being looted in the centre of town,' Robin said. 'The Brigands have set the tone, now everyone else is kicking off.'

'People will be scared to go out and vote.' Ísbjörg sighed. 'Especially in an hour, when it starts getting dark.'

Ísbjörg was still reading her email, and suddenly changed the subject. 'You've got a savings account with money, right?'

'I might,' Robin said coyly.

'Can you get three hundred in cash?'

Robin dug out his wallet to see what he had. 'I've got a cash card. But who's after my money?' he asked suspiciously.

'This email is from Neo Scarlock,' Emma explained, holding up her phone. 'He knows a guy, who knows a guy, who works as caretaker at Locksley Central benefits office, a couple of kilometres from here. The caretaker says the office is being used as a polling station. Says Gisborne's people showed up about 2pm and stuffed twenty ballot boxes with fake votes.'

'Twenty!' Robin said. 'Why so many?

'It's near the bus terminal, in front of that massive Freud Park housing estate,' Ísbjörg explained. 'I suppose a lot of people go there to vote. Neo says the caretaker will let us in to swap the votes, but he wants three hundred bucks.'

'Will I get my money back?'

Ísbjörg shrugged. 'I wouldn't count on that. But it is for your dad's election campaign.'

'Fine, I'm in,' Robin said reluctantly, as Sam opened the driver's side door and got in with three cardboard food boxes and a tray of drinks.

'Lucky we ordered now,' Sam said, as he checked inside a greasy box and handed it to Ísbjörg. 'The manager told me he's closing at six because they're expecting trouble tonight.'

'So hungry,' Robin said happily as he took his food and bit a huge chunk out of a hot wing.

Robin was still in the back stuffing his face a few minutes later when Sam tossed his burger wrapper behind his seat and set off to find a cash machine.

Much of central Locksley was derelict, but one of the few things that thrived were shops selling junk food and alcohol. Sam spotted a cash machine at the side of Best Price Beer, a store with barred windows and a double-gated entry designed to trap shoplifters and stick-up artists, and turned into its car park.

The other two buildings on the lot were rubble. There were five homeless people huddled against the wall near the cash machine, and a well-dressed teen with his cap on backwards who was surely selling drugs.

'Sketchy area to be pulling out money,' Sam said warily, looking back at Robin. 'Best if you stay out of sight and give me your card. Ísbjörg, keep your gun handy, just in case.'

'Do I trust you?' Robin asked as he handed Sam the card. 'PIN is 1454.'

Sam laughed as he read the name on Robin's card aloud. 'Mr Dick Long.'

'If I use my own name, the feds will freeze it,' Robin explained.

Sam's grin evaporated as he walked to the cash machine at the side of Best Price Beer. The ground was littered with syringes and the little foil strips that dealers used to wrap rocks of crack cocaine. Out on the road something was approaching, fast and noisy.

'Can you spare a little cash, young man?' one homeless woman asked.

Sam felt sorry for her. It looked like she'd taken a recent beating, and her sneakers and sleeping bag were black with filth.

He got the machine to check the balance on Robin's account to make sure there was £300 to withdraw. The answer on screen shocked him:

**£217,910.04**

'Holy smoke!' Sam gasped, then made a split-second decision to withdraw the maximum £500.

As the machine counted notes, the noise on the road grew until a convoy of three double-decker Locksley city buses went past at ground-shaking speed. The lead bus had all its downstairs windows smashed out. The second had rap music blasting and teenagers partying on the upper deck, while the third drove on the wrong side of the road, belching black diesel smoke as it tried to overtake.

'That won't end well,' the homeless woman observed, then smiled as Sam handed her £20.

Sam gave the four other homeless people £20 each. He urged them not to spend it on booze and drugs, then jogged back to the van.

'What was going on on those buses?' Ísbjörg asked as Sam got back inside.

'Kids must have stolen them from the transit depot at Central,' Robin said. 'And thanks for being so generous with *my* money.'

Robin was surprised by Sam's scowl as he handed the card back.

'There you go, Dick Long.'

'What?' Robin asked.

'I spent *my* last thirty pounds on Thunderbird Chicken, while you're sitting on an account with two hundred grand in it.'

'How did you get two hundred thousand?' Ísbjörg asked. 'I heard you lost the money you stole from cash machines when the mall burned down.'

'I was bored in Geography class,' Robin explained.

Sam and Ísbjörg laughed.

'How *exactly*?' Sam asked.

Robin sighed, like the answer was too obvious. 'I got my hands on a Locksley police staff database. Then I sent every cop a phishing email, pretending to be the police pension fund and asking them to confirm all their financial information. They were surprisingly gullible, considering they work in law enforcement.'

Ísbjörg had programmed the location of the council offices into the van's satnav, but Sam had to wait for a police convoy to pass before getting back on the road.

'That's not good,' Ísbjörg said ominously as three vanloads of cops in riot gear shot past, followed by two monstrous riot control vehicles fitted with water cannons and battering rams.

# 16. RED-HOT SPLINTER

17:17

Locksley's main benefits office was a six-floor block, running the length of a concrete precinct between the two tallest towers of the massive Freud Park housing estate. Sam cruised along the front of the precinct, where a launderette was the only outlet not boarded up and a queue of about a hundred voters shuffled forward.

'Two cops on duty,' Ísbjörg noted, glancing out of the passenger side.

A couple of volunteers tried to stay cheerful as they handed out *Vote Ardagh* badges, but the local Gisborne contingent were outdoing them. They'd set up a market stall with badges, stickers, free coffee and mini muffins with pictures of Guy Gisborne on top.

The trash chutes in Freud Park's two tower blocks were notorious for getting blocked. Rather than walk up to twenty floors with bags of rubbish, many residents lobbed them from their balconies into a stinking mound in the car park behind the benefits office.

Robin saw rats darting across the deserted parking lot as Sam let him out the back of the van. The caretaker was waiting for them by a rear entrance. A spindly man with an odd manner, he took his £300 straight away, but made them stand around holding bags stuffed with votes while he finished a small cigar.

Then the caretaker took them up to the first floor, through a maze of corridors with rows of identical office doors and into a room where twenty-one black metal ballot boxes were stacked on a meeting table.

An electoral official was in the room, using a hand trolley to deliver the latest full box from the voting area in the building's front reception.

'May I help you?' she asked, polite but stern. 'This room is for election officials only.'

'Wrong door, sorry!' the caretaker blurted as he backed out. 'We won't clean in here today.'

The woman gave Robin a look as she left the room, making sure the door was locked, then heading off pushing her squeaky-wheeled trolley. He hoped she was looking at his mad furry hat, rather than the face inside it.

They hid around the corner in a lift lobby until the woman was gone. Then the caretaker unlocked the office and let them in.

'No point me hanging around – you can see yourselves out.'

'Creepy bloke,' Robin said once the caretaker was out of earshot.

Ísbjörg nodded in agreement. 'His cigar smelled like old boots.'

'You two get to work,' Sam said. 'I'll keep lookout.'

'We'll keep this simple,' Ísbjörg told Robin as she handed Sam her silenced pistol. 'We won't sort votes. Just open each box and stuff as many of ours on top as you can.'

Robin popped the lid off the first box and began packing it with handfuls of fakes from a bin liner. Three minutes later he had two boxes to go when Sam leaned into the room making a cutting gesture.

'People coming up the front stairs. Let's scoot.'

Robin rapidly fixed the metal lid back on his box, but Ísbjörg's hand slipped while doing the same. She'd packed in too many votes, and papers sprang up and spilled across the carpet.

'Hurry up!' Sam warned as Robin dived to the floor and helped Ísbjörg pick up the votes, including a couple he had to retrieve from under a radiator.

As they exited the meeting room, Sam was gesturing frantically. A man had turned into the hallway.

'Excuse me! What were you doing in there?' he asked loudly. The man took his phone out to make a call as Robin, Sam and Ísbjörg ran.

'Balls, balls, balls!' Sam moaned as he leaped down a flight of stairs.

'Did we come up these stairs?' Robin asked his boots squeaking on the shiny steps.

'Sure,' Sam said, then added, 'Maybe . . . It all looks the same.'

At the bottom they found locked double doors.

'I told you it was Robin Hood!' shouted a woman upstairs. 'He's got a stupid hat on, but I could still tell.'

'I thought this hat was rather fetching,' Robin joked as they bombed it back up the stairs.

'Now which way?' Ísbjörg asked as she reached the top.

'No idea,' Sam said, but there were footsteps coming from one direction so they went in the other.

After thirty metres and a left turn, Robin glanced out of a little window and saw the car park with the massive trash pile on the far side. 'This is where we came in!' he said happily. 'Down the next stairs and we're out.'

But when they got to the bottom, the door had been sealed with a heavy-duty bike lock.

'Dirtbag,' Sam gasped, as he pounded the door in frustration.

'I knew there was something iffy about that caretaker,' Ísbjörg said.

There was another set of double doors behind them, but when Sam opened them he saw four huge blokes charging down the hallway towards them, and the footsteps on the next floor were closing in too.

Robin had left his bow in the van because carrying it around made his identity obvious. But he did have his backpack, and he knew that among all the junk he had a tin with the plastic explosive he used when he wanted an arrow to blow something up.

Sam opened the door and fired a couple of shots into the hallway ceiling, shattering a row of fluorescent light tubes and hopefully making the thugs coming towards them back off.

Robin hadn't tidied his pack out in months, but luckily remembered that he kept the explosive zipped in a waterproof pouch, right at the bottom where Marion's little brothers wouldn't get their mitts on it.

'This is gonna make a huge bang,' Robin warned, pressing a peanut-sized wedge of plastic explosive into the frame of the locked outer door.

Robin only carried impact detonators, designed to explode when an arrow hits something. 'I need you to shoot this,' Robin told Sam, pushing the fingernail-sized detonator into the blob of explosive.

'A bullet could ricochet anywhere,' Sam warned, as footsteps hit the stairs over their heads.

'And the blast will probably blow our eardrums,' Robin said. 'I'm all ears if you have any better ideas.'

Someone was peering nervously down from above as Sam, Robin and Ísbjörg took cover under the staircase. As Robin shielded his ears, Sam shot a hole through the locked door, but missed the detonator by several centimetres. As two of Gisborne's thugs edged through the open door into the stairwell, Sam's second shot hit the detonator.

The explosion obliterated the door and sent Gisborne's men flying. Smoke filled the air and smouldering razor-sharp splinters blasted in every direction.

Robin yelled in pain as heat seared his face and a hot splinter pierced the back of his hand. Ísbjörg cried out and held her ear.

'Run,' Sam shouted.

Robin was in pain and his ear rang from the blast, but the smoke had cleared enough for him to spot and grab an automatic pistol that one of Gisborne's men had dropped. It was dark and smoky in the deserted parking lot, and the explosion had set off a clanging metal fire bell on the side of the building.

There were a couple of figures crouching amidst the smoke, probably cops. But the way to the van was clear, and Robin sprinted. Blood streaked down his hand as he reached the van and looked back, expecting to see Ísbjörg and Sam behind him.

But there was no sign of them.

Maybe they were hurt, maybe they'd got in a struggle with one of Gisborne's men, or maybe they'd been forced to run the other way into the building. Robin had no way of finding out. He knew he was on his own, with the smoke rapidly clearing and two cops nearby, who'd spot him once they felt brave enough to look up.

'Don't be locked,' Robin begged, as he tried opening the back of the van. 'Thank you.'

As the van door swung open he stuffed the pistol into his trouser pocket, then reached inside and grabbed his bow.

'Freeze!' someone shouted from behind.

Three cops in riot gear were running around from the front of the precinct, though only the middle one had a weapon ready.

Robin squatted behind the van for cover, then realised that with cops left and right and the building full of people out to get him, his only escape was towards the mounds of trash from the tower blocks.

With luck, nobody would shoot him in the back before he got there . . .

# 17. RETURN OF THE CHEATER

17:30

Robin made it to the trash mound, but almost wished he hadn't as he stumbled over maggots, dirty nappies, bags of dog crap and a thousand rotting takeout boxes. As he swatted flies out of his face, a new bag of rubbish crashed down from the fifteenth floor and landed with a whoosh a few metres away.

He fell once when trash bags shifted underfoot, but Robin made it out of the mound with the greasy remnants of a doner kebab stuck to his trousers.

With Freud Park's twenty-storey towers at Robin's back, the estate's low-rise blocks stretched down both sides of a shabby pedestrian avenue for hundreds of metres. Overhead, the sky was starting to get dark and the high-level walkways that zigzagged between blocks were decorated with gang signs and pairs of trainers dangling by their laces.

Robin didn't know the estate's layout, but figured the best thing was to move fast and put space between himself and the people chasing him. He rubbed his ringing right ear as he jogged between the two rows of housing blocks. All the streetlights were dead, so the only light escaped from people's apartments.

None of the ground-floor apartments seemed to be occupied, their windows and doors sealed with rusting metal grilles. After sixty metres Robin turned left onto a downward slope and ran through an echoing tunnel beneath homes. A signpost at the end offered *Underground Garages* next to a down arrow, and *Shops, Cinema and Library* straight ahead.

A shout came from a third-floor balcony. 'Who are you?' it demanded. 'Strangers are not welcome round here.'

Robin decided it was best to keep moving. The little row of shops he ran past were all burnt out and boarded up, but as he broke into another alleyway lined with deserted apartments, he saw two cops running up concrete steps to get a view, and a whole platoon of riot police piling out of a van.

He ducked behind a huge concrete post and took a shaky breath. There were cops up ahead and almost certainly more spreading through the estate behind him if he doubled back.

The underground garages on one of Locksley's worst housing estates didn't seem like the kind of place Robin wanted to be, but going down seemed like his only choice.

Then when he stepped through the door into a concrete stairwell that smelled of urine, he immediately heard boots splashing along puddled concrete below.

'More cops,' Robin gasped, spinning around, sure it would only be moments before an officer spotted him.

Robin backed up to a boarded shop front, hoping it might buy a few seconds to come up with a genius plan, but as he got close he noticed a chunky tinted glass door with the lower pane missing.

Robin squeezed through and was surprised to find himself at the bottom of some broad concrete steps. The carpet tiles squelched underfoot and the walls were covered with graffiti, but there was enough light to see an old sign that read:

**Welcome to D.H. Lawrence Library**

Robin felt relieved as he jogged up the steps, realising that the library was situated over the parade of derelict shops. There was graffiti, mouldy ceiling tiles and a lot of smashed glass, but although the library had been closed for years, a surprising amount of shelving and books remained intact, filling the air with the woody aroma of damp paper.

'Hello?' Robin said quietly, realising that the bookshelves he was walking past would give excellent cover if cops came in.

He briefly wondered what had happened to Sam and Ísbjörg as he ducked between shelves in the History of

Art section. He found a little wheeled library stool to sit on and pulled out his walkie-talkie.

'Hello, Control?'

Nothing came back.

'Control, this is AB19. Do you copy?' Robin worried that the rebels' radio network didn't work this far into Locksley, and also that the power was down to six per cent because he'd not charged his walkie-talkie overnight.

'AB19, this is Control,' the radio blared, much to Robin's relief. 'We've been monitoring police radio and we're worried about you. Are you safe and unharmed?'

'No injuries. I'm hiding in the abandoned library in the middle of Freud Park estate. But there's cops everywhere. They'll figure out where I am before long.'

'I hear you,' Control said. 'I'm going to speak to the team and discuss our options for getting you out of there.'

'Cool,' Robin said nervously. 'If my radio goes flat, I have my phone.'

'Stand by for an update, AB19.'

As Robin waited, he rummaged in his pack and gulped water from his canteen. Then he tore a page out of a chunky book on medieval art and used it to flick off some of the food and squirming maggots stuck to his trousers.

When his phone buzzed, Robin was surprised to see a goofy picture of his former best friend Alan Adale on screen. They'd barely spoken in weeks, and Robin answered irritably. 'What do you want?'

'Mate,' Alan began awkwardly. 'I know we've been avoiding each other since, you know . . .'

Robin grunted. 'Since I caught you snogging my girlfriend.'

'I wanted to run something by you, because you're good at saving-the-world type stuff,' Alan continued. 'Do you remember Tiffany Stalin, in our Year Seven class at Locksley High?'

'Sure,' Robin said, picturing a stuck-up girl who had teased him for wearing Little John's hand-me-down uniform and no-brand trainers.

'After you ran off and got famous, people thought I was cool, because I knew you. I wound up snogging Tiffany at the Christmas disco.'

'I'm a tad busy right now,' Robin said tersely, turning up his radio to make sure he didn't miss a message from Control. 'And to be honest, I wasn't into Locksley High gossip even when I was at Locksley High.'

Now Alan sounded irritated. 'I think I'm onto something really big,' he said. 'I called you because I still hardly know anyone at Sherwood Castle and all the important people are at the White House anyway.

'My point is, Tiffany took my number, but never messaged me – until today. She was crying her eyes out, asking if I could put her in touch with some rebels who can help her.

'She got home from school an hour ago. Her house was in a state, no sign of her mum or sister. The dog's run off, her dad's car was on the drive with the door open, and one of his shoes was halfway up the driveway, like someone had dragged him off.'

Robin scoffed. 'Rich guy, probably did something to piss off Gisborne.'

'But that's where things get really interesting,' Alan said, as Robin saw looming shadows near the library entrance. 'It turns out, Tiffany's dad is—'

'Alan, I gotta go,' Robin said,

He hung up, took his bow and notched an arrow. He peered through a gap in the mouldy art history books, and saw a pair of riot-helmeted cops walking down the library's main aisle towards him.

# 18. SERIAL KILLER

17:45

One cop squatted down and shone a torch. The beam of light fired beneath the bookshelves, lighting up a floor covered with crashed ceiling tiles and beer cans. Robin's hand trembled on the bow and he kept remembering the image of the wife and son of the last person he'd killed with an arrow.

*Maybe I'll surrender.*

*Can I shoot them?*

'Gotcha, turd!' an officer sang triumphantly when her beam caught Robin's boots. 'Stand up! Hands in the air.'

The second officer made Robin's decision easier. 'I can smell Gisborne's money,' she joked, as she closed in on Robin with her rifle ready to shoot.

So, Robin's choice wasn't 'surrender to the cops and get sent to jail' but 'surrender to the cops and get handed to psycho Gisborne and his massive whip collection'.

*Corrupt cops ruined this town . . .*

'Drop the arrow and stand up slow.'

Robin jerked sideways, around the narrow end of a bookshelf. The second officer shot twice, but even a high-velocity bullet won't pass longways through two metres of books.

Robin shot backwards, hopping across to hide behind the next rack of books, while firing an arrow into the vulnerable area between the base of the officer's helmet and the top of her body armour.

As the other officer took aim at his head, Robin fired through a gap in the art history books and hit her in the belly. When she cried out, Robin sprinted between the shelves and shot her in the back at point-blank range.

His moves were fast and clinical. But carbon fibre breaks into razor-sharp fragments when it hits bone. Blood was soaking from a large wound beneath the woman's body armour and she was coughing up blood inside her helmet.

'No choice,' Robin told himself firmly, but still felt like puking.

*Courier* headlines popped into his head:

**Evil Hood kills mother of six . . .**

There didn't seem to be any more cops in the library, but other officers had surely heard the rifle shots, or seen muzzle flashes through the library's grubby windows.

Robin felt shaky as he did what he had to: maximise his chance of escaping by arming himself with the pepper spray and stun gun clipped to the officer's belt. He also took the officer's radio, so he'd get to hear what the cops were up to, and stripped the body cameras from both officers. He didn't want that video getting online, especially if the cops got a chance to edit it first.

*Now where?*

Robin assumed there were now two vanloads of cops swarming Freud Park estate at ground level. Staying in the library wasn't an option, so he looked for a way onto the building's flat roof.

He quickly swung the officer's torch around at the ceiling. There were crumbling tiles and a ceiling fan dangled by its wiring, but no sign of a hatch that would let him onto the roof.

As Robin's attention turned to a line of big dirt-crusted windows at the rear of the library, the police radio burbled.

'Undetermined gunshot reported. All units, please check in. Begin, Unit 1.'

'Unit 1, checking in.'

'Unit 2, I'm alive, didn't hear anything,' another officer responded.

The windows seemed to slide down at the top. A rusty latch on the middle one took all Robin's strength to undo and as he tugged the glass panel down, strips of bright green moss dropped on his head.

The cops kept checking in until they got to Unit 16.

'Unit 16, do you copy?'

There was silence on the police radio. Robin dragged a table to below the window, then stood on it and stuck his head outside.

'What was the last reported sighting of Unit 16?'

'This is Unit 8. I sent 16 and 17 to search the library building.'

'Unit 17, do you copy?'

Robin saw the library's roof about thirty centimetres above the window. He balanced his boot on the window frame, then twisted around to grasp the edge.

As Robin pulled himself up onto the roof, the police controller came back on the radio, sounding worried. 'Officers 16 and 17 are non-responsive. I need everyone near the library to find them. Proceed with extreme caution. We know what Robin Hood is capable of.'

Robin tried to hide his escape route by reaching down and pulling up the window, but his arms weren't long enough. As he strained, he heard at least two sets of boots on the library stairs.

He ran sixty metres across the asphalt roof, taking in a view of a huge fire in the centre of town and a Channel 9 news helicopter in the air. At the end of the roof, Robin jumped down onto one of the graffiti-splattered walkways that spanned between the blocks.

As he ran, the police radio erupted. 'We found Units 16 and 17. Arrows through their body armour, alive but losing blood. Get an ambulance here ASAP.'

'Form a perimeter!' the police controller screamed furiously. 'The boss wants Robin alive, but I'm past caring. If you see that kid, shoot him.'

# 19. SHOOT TO KILL

17:57

Robin ran flat out, his pack thumping against his back and his bow sliding off his shoulder. When his phone started to vibrate, he slowed down to take it out of his pocket.

'Yeah,' Robin blurted.

'Heard you're in a pickle,' a youthful male voice said cheerfully. 'There's no rebels near you, so Control put out a call for help.'

The voice seemed familiar, but a background of throbbing motorbike engine made it hard to discern, and Robin figured introductions could wait.

'I'm riding – two minutes from Freud Park,' the biker said. 'Where are you exactly?'

'Walkway, running away from some old library,' Robin gasped as he glanced over the railings and saw two riot cops down at ground level. 'I think I'm heading north. There's cops everywhere.'

'I squatted a flat in Freud Park a while back,' the man said confidently. 'You need to break left when that walkway splits three ways. You'll run past a line of apartments. When you get near a dead end, you'll need to cross through one of the apartments. Then you can clamber down from the rear balcony and I'll meet you at the end of the alleyway.'

'*Through* an apartment,' Robin said, reaching the split in the walkway and cutting left. 'How do I do that?'

'Ring a doorbell? Break a window? You'll have to figure it out.'

'Great.' Robin groaned, knowing that Freud Park was an estate where people had been shot for straying onto the wrong gang's turf, let alone trying to force their way into an apartment.

As the dead end loomed, the first three apartments Robin passed had fire damage and heavy grilles over doors and windows. The fourth seemed hopeful, with a TV flickering inside. He rang the bell, but nobody was in any hurry to answer, so he hit the bell on the next flat too.

An elderly woman opened the door quickly, but kept a thick chain on to stop anyone forcing their way in. Robin heard a cop coming up some stairs he'd passed thirty metres back.

'I need to get through your flat and climb down from the balcony,' Robin said. 'It'll only take five seconds.'

'You're Robin Hood,' the woman said.

'I am,' Robin agreed, glancing back along the landing.

The cop must have spotted him, but the officer was being cautious and shielded his body behind the wall at the top of the staircase.

'I'm begging you to take that chain off your door and let me through. The cops are after me.'

'I voted for your father. He seems like a nice man.'

'He is,' Robin agreed, as a powerful lamp shone from the ground and lit up his back. '*Please* let me in. They're gonna kill me.'

The cop by the stairs came over the radio. 'I can confirm I have identified Hood and have a clean shot. Control, please confirm the order to take him out.'

The old lady started to take the chain off her door, but she had arthritis and her hands were slow. The guy in the flat next door finally opened his door and stepped out onto the walkway. He was bare-chested and had a giant Macondo United tattoo on his back.

'All units are clear to shoot!' the police controller said, but now the neighbour was in the way.

'Get back inside!' the cop crouching at the top of the stairs shouted. 'Police!'

As the big man freaked out and leaped back into his flat, the old lady finally got the chain off.

'Sorry,' Robin said, knocking her into the wall as he barged in.

The flat was cosy. There was a little kitchen that opened into a living area, with shelves of old photographs and a collection of china dolls.

'Your boots!' the old lady said, as Robin trailed sticky garbage across her rug.

'So sorry,' Robin said, scrambling past the TV and unlocking the sliding glass door onto a balcony covered with plant pots. 'I'll send you money. You can buy twenty rugs.'

*If I make it out of here alive.*

Robin looked over the balconies and saw a three-floor drop to a narrow, unlit alleyway. Each balcony jutted out further than the one above, making the climb easy.

'You mind yourself,' the old lady warned as Robin swung his leg over the balcony railing.

He dropped, swung and repeated until he was down at ground level in a pitch-dark alleyway choked with rubbish bags, a rusty bed frame and mounds of rubble sacks.

'Robin Hood!' someone shouted, as he stumbled over it all.

As Robin broke out of the alleyway, he saw a biker. He wore the colours of the Liverpool chapter of Brigands Motorcycle Club and sat astride a very impressive Harley Davidson. Robin finally put a name to the voice on the end of the phone. It was Marion's oldest brother.

'Flash,' Robin gasped, then glanced around nervously as he straddled the bike. 'I was two seconds from getting my head blown off up there. You totally saved my arse.'

'Hold tight,' Flash said, and he opened the bike's throttle and blasted off.

With no helmet, Robin's hair was going crazy and he could barely keep his eyes open, but he still managed to peek over Flash's shoulder at the road ahead. Robin was so stunned by what he saw tied between the handlebars that he wondered if the stressful escape had fused his brain.

'Is that a crib?' Robin blurted as his eyes locked on a tiny yawning baby.

# 20. FLO'S CAFF

18:15

As Flash's bike sped along, Robin wondered if Sam and Ísbjörg were OK, and whether the ambulance coming the other way was for the two women he'd shot.

Locksley streets felt super edgy now it was dark. They sped past gangs of young men looking for trouble. Every business was shuttered and one row of shops had business owners lined up behind wheelie bins with bats and shotguns, ready to defend their property from looters.

Robin felt conspicuous on the back of a noisy chromed bike, racing through deserted streets with the bow hanging off his shoulder making his identity obvious. Flash clearly knew this too, so after a five-minute blast away from Freud Park he parked in a line of Harley Davidsons behind Flo's Cafe.

It was an old-school fried-breakfast joint that was mostly frequented by bikers. The shutters were down, but light shone through gaps around the edges.

'I'll be two minutes,' Flash told Robin, as he pounded on the shutter.

As someone half opened the shutter so that Flash could duck inside, Robin's adrenaline dropped enough for him to notice the ringing in his ears and think about the painful charred wood splinter jutting three centimetres from the back of his hand.

Blood was crusting around the wound, but he decided not to pull out the splinter until he had better light and something to wrap over it. Then he looked up at the crib strapped between the handlebars and remembered that the last time he'd seen Flash, his girlfriend Agnes had been pregnant.

'We got wheels,' Flash said, when he came out jangling a set of car keys.

'What about your bike?' Robin asked.

'It would take a brave looter to come near a line of Brigand bikes.'

'Who's the little one?' Robin asked, as Flash ripped off the Velcro strips holding the crib in place.

'Holly Maid,' Flash said proudly, tilting the crib so Robin got a better look.

'She's tiny.'

'Five weeks old. Her mother's having a hard time adjusting. So she's with me most of the time. Car is this way.'

Flash held the crib, and all the gear Robin had stripped from the two cops rattled as they strode a couple of hundred metres. Their ride was a sporty little Audi hatchback with a matt black paint job.

'Belongs to a biker called Titty,' Flash explained. 'Nice guy, but he says he'll cut off my toes and feed them to his pit bull if I scratch it.'

Robin half smiled as he climbed in the back, then shuffled across so that Holly's crib could slide onto the seat beside him. Flash used Robin's backpack as a wedge to stop her sliding about.

Robin was so used to riding around hidden in the back of a van, or the filthy trunk of some tatty car, that the Audi's comfy leather seats and fancy LED interior lights felt like some sleek alien spaceship.

'How come you're back in town?' Robin asked as Flash pulled out from the kerb. 'Last I heard, you stole twenty thousand from Sherwood Forest Brigands and only made it out of town alive because their leader Cut-Throat is your dad.'

'I wasn't the most popular kid in town for a while,' Flash agreed. 'But me and Agnes learned your old trick: hacking cash machines.'

'Seriously?' Robin said. 'I thought they'd taken all the vulnerable QT3.14s out of service.'

'Gang in Holland developed a technique for newer machines,' Flash said, smirking proudly. 'I might even be able to teach the great Robin Hood a thing or two now.'

'Probably could,' Robin agreed, though in truth Robin's hacking mentor D'Angela had since taught him skills that made plugging wires into some grubby cash machine to make a measly thousand bucks seem primitive.

'Me and Agnes hit cash machines hard, mostly in France and Spain. I set enough aside to bring Holly up right, then I paid my debts to Sherwood Forest Brigands with generous interest.'

'I'm surprised they forgave you,' Robin said. 'Bikers don't like getting ripped off, even if you pay them back.'

Flash smiled awkwardly as he turned onto a main road. 'A lot of Sherwood Brigands still hate my guts, but most of those guys are permanently broke and needed the money.'

After eight minutes of sensible driving, Flash turned into the parking lot of a Fireside Motel. Robin had never stayed in one, but he remembered the brand's TV commercials, with wholesome families jumping on crisp white bed linen and its *You'll get a warm welcome at Fireside* slogan.

Reality was less shiny than the ads, with the exterior's peeling paint, dead lightbulbs and vending machines with *out of order* signs.

'I'll park directly outside our room. You run straight inside so nobody sees. Then I'll get Holly and your stuff.'

Robin unlocked the motel room and caught a musty smell as he flipped on the light. The room had two double beds, and the number of pizza boxes and beer cans littering the place suggested that Flash had been staying for a while. He also noticed a big pack of nappies and other stuff for Holly, but no sign of clothes or toiletries belonging to the baby's mum.

'Nice wheels, man,' a cocky lad shouted across the parking lot as Flash slid Holly's crib out of the Audi.

Robin peeked around the edge of a blind and watched four young lads swaggering towards Flash. Robin's bow was still on the back seat of the car, but he had pepper spray in his hoodie pocket and the handgun he'd snatched at the benefits office.

The lads looked no older than sixteen, but two of them brandished baseball bats as they moved in.

'Gimme them keys, bruv!' one yelled.

'We'll bring it back, we promise,' another joked.

Flash played it cool, turning slowly and resting Holly's crib on the car roof. The four lads froze the instant they saw the Brigands Liverpool logo on the back of Flash's leather jacket.

'Sir, we didn't . . .' one stuttered, as he remembered the code of honour that gives bike gangs their fearsome reputation: lay a finger on one biker, their whole gang comes after you.

'No disrespect,' another added, starting to walk backwards.

'You're lucky I've got my baby here,' Flash growled. He made a *go away* gesture with his free hand. The lads wouldn't have run any faster if he'd shot bullets at them.

Robin laughed as Flash brought the rest of the stuff inside and double-locked the door.

'You'd better clean up that manky hand,' Flash said, as he leaned over Holly's little crib to make sure she was still sleeping. 'Use the antiseptic cream in my wash bag. I don't got any bandage, but there's a bandana you can use in my suitcase.'

Robin found the bandana, then tripped over a pair of Flash's jeans as he stepped into the bathroom. He rested his phone on the sink and looked at himself in the mirror. His hair was matted and his T-shirt drenched in sweat. Mud, blood, bin juice and bird crap covered his clothes.

The ringing from the explosion had stopped, but Robin's hand was painful and would hurt more in a second when he pulled out the splinter. The weirdest thing was that he felt different than he normally did.

Robin had always been a thrill seeker who thrived on danger and buzzed with excitement after doing something dangerous. But today he just felt queasy as he washed the blood off his hand.

He worried about Sam and Ísbjörg, wondered if the two cops he'd shot were parents, and freaked out recalling how close he'd come to having a police marksman splatter his brains over a third-floor balcony.

Robin took a long breath and slowly shook his head.

'I'm getting too old for this,' the thirteen-year-old told himself.

# 21. A MILLION SPLINTERS

18:43

When Robin came out of the bathroom with a stars and stripes bandana wrapped around his hand, Flash was sitting on the edge of his bed giving Holly a bottle and murmuring, 'Good girl, good girl,' as she fed.

'Will I disturb her if I flick on the news?' Robin asked.

'You won't mind, will you, sweetie?' Flash said softly. Then to Robin, 'I let Rebel Control know you're safe and I plugged your walkie-talkie into my laptop charger.'

'Cheers,' Robin said, surprised by this gentle side to Flash, which he'd not seen before.

'Everyone's busy with election stuff. And nobody's gonna come looking for you here, so Control says it's best if you stick here until things calm down.'

'Makes sense,' Robin said, as he crashed on the other bed and grabbed the remote. 'I'm wiped out anyway.'

The Fireside Motel's TV was a tiny box mounted near the ceiling, with only five channels. Robin found a local bulletin on Channel 9. And while the media had taken no interest in the vote-rigging rumours earlier in the day, trouble on the Locksley streets with barricades, police chases and cars on fire was the kind of drama that TV news loves.

'At least one teenager was killed when a stolen bus lost control and crashed into an electricity pylon,' the newscaster said. 'While fire engines have been called in from neighbouring counties to try and deal with a huge fire at the Locksley Transit Museum, which is believed to have been started deliberately by girls on a Year Nine field trip . . .'

As the newsreader catalogued more horrors in Locksley, Robin unlocked his phone and checked his messages. The two most recent were from Marion Maid and Sam Scarlock. He checked the message from Sam first:

Heard you're safe! So relieved.
My shooting arm took a million splinters
when that door blew up, but Ísbjörg helped
me escape through reception. Now back
at Sherwood Castle clinic, for fun times
getting splinters pulled out!

Robin quickly replied, **glad you're OK**, then he touched Marion's name and saw that she'd messaged him several times in the last hour and a bit.

> **17:24**
> Why did you hang up on Alan? It's important. Call me when you get this.
> **17:46**
> Forget last message, heard you're in trouble. LOVE YOU, stay safe!
> **18:38**
> Glad you're safe. Still need help. Everyone busy at Ardagh HQ. Please call if you can.

Robin hit the button to call Marion, and she picked up instantly.

'Robin! They said you're safe, but I've got no idea where you are.'

'I'm in a motel, with your big brother.'

'Flash?' Marion said disbelievingly. 'You can't be. Our dad will kill him if he comes anywhere near Locksley.'

'Things change,' Robin said. 'He's right here. I can put you on speaker.'

'Yes . . . Actually, no. I need to tell you this thing about Alan and Tiffany Stalin first. How far did Alan get with the story?'

Robin struggled to remember. 'Some gossip about Tiffany coming home from school. Family gone, house trashed.'

'That's right,' Marion said.

'Why should I care?' Robin asked casually. 'People are kidnapped all the time if they get on the wrong side of Gisborne.'

'Tiffany's dad isn't super rich. Mr Stalin is a senior administrator for the county. Tonight, he's a returning officer for Nottingham and everywhere east of the city. That's half the people in the county.'

'What's a returning officer?'

'Tiffany explained it to me,' Marion said. 'When the polls close at nine-thirty, two returning officers are responsible for ensuring that all votes are collected from polling stations, delivered to one of two counting centres and added up properly. Then one of the returning officers announces who the next sheriff is going to be at Locksley town hall.'

'You're kidding!' Robin moaned, now that he understood. 'We've spent all day stuffing ballot boxes, but it doesn't matter because Gisborne has kidnapped the guy in charge of adding the votes up?'

'You've been vote-stuffing in Locksley and the west,' Marion said. 'Mr Stalin is responsible for counting the votes in Nottingham and the east.'

'What's being done about it?' Robin asked. 'What did Will and Emma say?'

Marion gave a deep sigh. 'I called them before I called you, but everyone is swamped. Will and Emma are on their way to Nottingham and haven't replied to my messages. Azeem and the rest of the security teams are spread all over because Gisborne's henchmen have been beating up our campaigners and trashing our buses. Sam's in the clinic. Neo and Ten Man got pulled over by cops and Tybalt the lawyer is trying to get them out before they're shipped off to Pelican Island. The only people left at headquarters are the volunteers who cook food and this random old hippy who says I need to calm down and meditate.'

'Down to us then.' Robin groaned. 'As usual.'

Marion sounded surprised. 'You spend half your life trying to get out of school and do something exciting. Now it's all kicking off and you're moaning?'

'It's been a long day and I almost got my head blown off,' Robin explained. 'But it'll take more than us two to find out what Gisborne's done with Tiffany's family.'

'And it's almost seven now,' Marion said. 'Polling stations close in just over two hours.'

Robin glanced across the room at Flash. 'The bikers don't want Gisborne elected any more than we do,' he told Marion. 'Maybe your brother and some of his biker chums can help.'

# 22. KANGAROO COURTS

19:25

The smell of smoke seemed to be everywhere as Flash drove the Audi ten kilometres north to Queen's View.

While central Locksley had deteriorated, this neighbourhood provided modern homes with pools and air conditioning. Most people who could afford to live here either worked for Guy Gisborne or had well-paying government jobs where they kept on the gangster's good side if they didn't want to end up wearing concrete shoes at the bottom of the Macondo River.

'It's that house,' Robin said, bobbing up from his hiding spot across the back seat and pointing. 'Number fifty-seven.'

Robin had been here hundreds of times to hang out with his former best friend, Alan. The place stirred fond memories of sleepovers and water fights, but now the house was unoccupied.

Alan lived with the rebels at Sherwood Castle, Alan's mum had abandoned her family for a job in Capital City, his sister Dakota lived with an auntie, and his dad had skipped town after falling out with Gisborne.

'Hello?' Robin said, as he stepped through the unlocked front door and peered into the kitchen.

Doors had been ripped off the wall cabinets and everything was dusty, but the basket of dirty laundry and dishes in the sink suggested that Alan's dad had left in a hurry.

Marion strode out from the living area. She gave Robin a hug, but backed off fast. 'Glad you're OK, but have you heard of deodorant?'

'I'm hardly gonna smell like roses after the day I've had,' Robin said grumpily. 'Did you get here OK?'

Marion shrugged. 'Alan and me rode dirt bikes from headquarters. It's scary driving through town, but we lived to tell the tale.'

Now Flash walked in, holding Holly in her crib.

'Kevin,' Marion said, teasing Flash with the real name he hated. 'Eww! Is that a baby?'

'Holly,' Flash told his infant daughter sarcastically. 'This is your Auntie Marion. She hides her sweet nature behind a wall of hostility. But some day she'll love you very much.'

'Don't bet on that,' Marion scoffed, but she couldn't fully disguise her smile as she peered into the crib and gently squashed her five-week-old niece's nose. 'Boop!'

Alan came out from the lounge and shook Flash's hand, but only exchanged a wary glance with Robin. Robin said hi to Tiffany as he joined her in the unlit lounge. She sat awkwardly on the arm of a sofa, biting a thumbnail and wearing a purple Locksley High polo shirt.

'The good news is, Will *finally* got my message,' Marion told Robin.

'The rumour going round is that Locksley police are switching off chunks of the mobile network to stop troublemakers communicating,' Alan explained.

'Will's taking the threat seriously,' Marion said. 'He'll try to send back-up to help us out. But everyone's busy and with phones cutting out and people blockading streets to protect their neighbourhoods from rioters, don't expect them any time soon.'

'So, Tiffany,' Robin said, feeling awkward to be helping someone he'd always thought of as a snobby bully. 'Your house is near here?'

'Literally next street across,' Tiffany said, sounding stressed and close to crying. 'If you go upstairs, you can see our pool over the back fence.'

'I knew this old place was empty,' Alan explained. 'I told Tiffany to hide here, in case Gisborne's people come looking.'

'Why didn't they kidnap you with your mum and sister?' Flash asked.

'Most days I leave early and go for a smoothie with Beth and Steph. Then we share a taxi to Locksley High.'

*Taxi!* Robin thought irritably. He remembered Tiffany, Bethany and Stephanie spending a whole day calling him Mr Squelch when his trainers got soaked after he ran to school in a thunderstorm.

'On any other day, I bet one of Gisborne's goons would have had someone waiting to pick Tiffany up when she got out of school,' Marion said. 'But with all the election stuff going on, I guess they're at full stretch.'

'Just a thought,' Alan said hesitantly. 'I know we want Ardagh to win the election. But what if we let this play out? If Tiffany's dad does exactly what he's told, why wouldn't Gisborne let the family go?'

'I'm not sure,' Tiffany said. 'My family has been on Gisborne's blacklist for a while. Daddy always said he was lucky because he works for the voter registration department in Nottingham, not here in Locksley. Until Gisborne decided to run for sheriff, he never got involved with Gisborne's people.

'Then last year my Uncle Joe got his arm crushed in a faulty compactor at one of Gisborne's trash dumps. Gisborne said it was my uncle's fault and refused to give him sick pay or injury compensation. So my dad lent Joe some money to hire a lawyer . . .'

Robin and Flash gasped.

'They tried to sue Gisborne, in a Locksley court?' Flash blurted.

'That's crazy!' Robin added. 'Gisborne owns every judge in town.'

Tiffany sounded tearful. 'Mummy *told* him it was suicidal. But Daddy and Uncle Joe were really angry and they thought Gisborne would offer to settle the case, just to get them off his back. Instead, Gisborne went psycho and started making trouble for us.'

'What happened in court?' Robin asked.

'It never got there.' Tiffany snorted. 'The lawyer my uncle hired was another *friend* of Gisborne. He did everything super slow, messed up all the court paperwork and kept asking for more money until we gave up.

'At the same time, Daddy started getting bullied by his boss and the payroll department kept messing about, so he either didn't get paid or the amount was way short. Mummy and Daddy have been trying to sell our house and find jobs in another town, but that's hard. If you're from Locksley, everyone assumes you're a crook.'

'Gisborne's got *everything* in this town locked down,' Flash said bitterly.

'I'm glad you all came here to help,' Tiffany said. 'But how do we even start to help my family? They could be a hundred kilometres away by now.'

'What about your dad?' Robin asked. 'It's election day, so shouldn't he be at work?'

'Daddy's job is to supervise the counting of votes and announce the result. I think he was going in to work about an hour before polls close,' Tiffany explained. 'He had plans to play squash with a friend this morning.'

'Well, at least we know your dad has to be at the town hall later on,' Marion pointed out.

Tiffany looked at Robin. 'Our house has a video doorbell. The only clue I've got is some footage of guys dragging Daddy into a van. But the men are wearing masks and you can't read the licence plate of the van.'

Robin sounded curious. 'Can I watch it? I might be able to do something.'

'It's blurry as,' Alan warned, as Tiffany opened the doorbell app on her phone and passed it to Robin. 'There's probably not much point.'

'There's a couple of things I could look at online,' Robin said, as he keenly watched and rewatched the clip of Ken Stalin being dragged into a tatty white van, dressed in shorts and tennis shoes. 'My laptop is back at Sherwood Castle, so I'm gonna need a computer with a keyboard and a decent internet connection.'

'My sister Dakota's old laptop is in her room,' Alan said, as he raced for the stairs. 'They haven't cut electricity off yet, but phone and internet are dead.'

Marion checked the data speed on her phone. 'I've got fifty megabits and forty per cent battery. As long as the mobile network doesn't get switched off . . .'

'We can tether the laptop,' Robin said eagerly. 'Go to settings, communication, turn on Wi-Fi hotspot.'

'I know,' Marion said irritably.

When Alan came back downstairs holding a kiddies' laptop with a rubbery purple shell, Tiffany sounded confused. 'I don't understand what you can get from that video clip,' she said.

Robin had sympathy for Tiffany now he'd heard her story, but he still spoke bluntly. 'I can spend ten minutes explaining. Or ten minutes logging into my hacking tools and getting on with it.'

# 23. BLURRY WHITE VAN

19:33

The knackered kiddies' laptop took ages to boot, then it took several painful minutes for Robin to bypass Dakota Adale's password. Once online, he copied a bunch of login details off his phone, giving him a connection to the Super back at Sherwood Castle.

The Super was a powerful machine, whose artificial intelligence engine was linked to vast quantities of stolen personal data and hacked links to over a thousand live data sources. As Flash, Marion, Alan and Tiffany loomed over Robin's shoulder, Robin typed a natural language query:

**Show me Locksley police cameras near 57 Albert Road. Then put the locations on a map.**

The Super was smart enough to interpret this information, log into Locksley police's camera system and build a map showing the location of all the police cameras near Alan's former home.

'I didn't know hacking was this easy,' Tiffany said.

'It's not,' Robin said. 'Every information source in the Super's data lake took hours of work to hack. You're just looking at the end result. And can you guys step back? I can't work with you breathing down my neck.'

'Lots of ANPR cameras around here,' Flash noted. 'I had no idea there were so many.'

'What's ANPR?' Tiffany asked.

'Automatic Number Plate Recognition,' Robin answered. 'It means the camera filming cars reads registration plates and tips off the cops if it detects a stolen car or something.'

'We've got cameras because most senior cops live here,' Alan explained.

'It's true,' Tiffany agreed. 'They say Locksley has the highest crime in the country, but nobody gets burgled in Queen's View.'

'Remind me, what's the time stamp on that doorbell clip?' Robin asked.

'Eight-seventeen,' Tiffany answered.

Robin clicked the camera icons on the map and asked the Super to replay footage from that morning. A camera in the next street had picked up a white van passing by at 08:04, then going back in the other direction at 08:20.

'That's the one,' Marion said, as she leaned closer to the little laptop screen. 'It's got that grey smudge on the side. Like an old logo that's been painted over.'

Robin typed in the registration KNY 130 77 and asked the Super to check it against ANPR cameras, crime reports and vehicle databases.

```
KNY 130 77
Vehicle type: Peugeot 208
Colour: Green
Owner: Grace Wong, 27 Laird Street,
Edinburgh
```

'That's not a green Peugeot,' Marion noted. 'Did you type it in wrong?'

'Nah,' Robin said. 'I bet they fitted the van with a copy of someone else's licence plate. But we can still tell which other police cameras picked up that number plate in Locksley today.'

The Super found several ANPR hits, showing the white van heading a couple of kilometres east after it left Tiffany's driveway.

'That camera is across the street from my brother's school,' Tiffany said. 'And 08:53 is exactly when my mum would have been dropping Joe off.'

Robin nodded. 'There might be CCTV cameras in the school I can hack into, but for now let's assume Gisborne's goons drove to your brother's school, where they kidnapped your mum and brother.'

'Why didn't they arrive earlier and pick us all up while we were still home?' Tiffany asked.

Robin thought for a moment. 'Gisborne's smart. He would have planned this carefully, but some of his muscle men aren't exactly geniuses. My guess is the two goons arrived at your house late. They caught your dad just before he left to play squash, then they chased down your mum and brother on the way to school.'

Robin looked disappointed when he saw that the next two hits on ANPR cameras showed the van heading out of Locksley on a country road. 'There aren't many ANPR cameras once you leave the city.'

'So, my family are probably being held in some remote house, west of town.' Tiffany sighed. 'But that's not much help.'

Robin scanned down the list of ANPR hits. The van had briefly been driven in and out of town in the middle of the day, but more interestingly the system had picked it up re-entering Locksley just twenty minutes ago.

'Looks like the van is heading west back into town.'

'I bet it's taking my dad into town to start work,' Tiffany said, but she looked surprised when she saw the van's route. 'Except my dad is supposed to be working in the counting room at Locksley town hall, and the van has passed the turn-off and kept going north.'

'Back here?' Marion suggested.

Robin thought for a couple of seconds. 'You said your dad was playing squash, right?'

Tiffany instantly realised what Robin was getting at. 'When they kidnapped Daddy, they were in a big rush and he was dressed for the fitness centre. But my dad will need to have his work phone and his briefcase, so they're taking him back here.'

'Cool!' Flash said excitedly.

'Why's it cool?' Marion asked. 'I mean, how does it help us?'

Tiffany sobbed. 'I might never see Mummy again.'

Robin drummed his fingers on the laptop, trying to think. 'If we can get in touch with your dad somehow, he might be able to tell us where your mum and brother are being held.'

'Unless they blindfolded him,' Marion noted.

'And he might not have seen much from the back of a van,' Alan added.

'True,' Robin said. 'Or, what if we could somehow identify the men who've been holding him hostage? If we could steal one of their smartphones somehow, there would be tons of information.'

'How about I stick a gun in their faces and threaten to blow their heads off?' Flash suggested, pounding a fist into his palm.

'Don't be daft, Kevin.' Marion tutted. 'If Tiffany's dad doesn't show up at Locksley town hall on time and with his minders, Gisborne will know something's wrong and Tiffany's family will be toast.'

Tiffany sobbed again.

'We'll think of something,' Marion said, putting her arm around Tiffany.

'Whatever we come up with, it better be fast.' Robin sighed as another ANPR camera detected the van. 'That van will be at Tiffany's house in ten minutes.'

# 24. IN THE CAN

19:56

As the white van rolled onto the front drive of the Stalin family home, Tiffany and Marion scrambled out through the home's rear patio doors and raced around the swimming pool to the fence at the back of the garden.

Marion vaulted the fence easily, but Alan had to reach over from the other side to pull Tiffany up.

Back around the front of Tiffany's home, Robin and Flash squatted in a wheelie bin store as they watched one of Gisborne's goons get out the front of the van. He was unmasked and looked uncomfortable in a suit that was way too tight.

'Van wasn't that dirty earlier,' Flash whispered. 'It's been off-road.'

The goon walked to the back of the van and let out Tiffany's dad, Ken Stalin.

'Think about messing around and I'll have Sandra cut your boy's thumbs off,' the goon warned chillingly.

Ken cut a pathetic figure, with long skinny legs in white shorts and a bloodstain down his white polo shirt from a punch in the nose.

'I understand,' Ken said shakily, as he got shoved towards his front door.

Once the pair were inside, Robin crept up to the van to make sure there were no other passengers, then peered into the kitchen through the bay window at the front of the house.

Robin heard Ken shout. 'Tiffany? Princess? Are you home?'

Robin realised the home had the same floorplan as Alan's place in the next street. Then he ducked as the kitchen lights flicked on. When he peeked again, the two men were heading upstairs and out of earshot.

# 25. TIFF'S REBEL FRIENDS

20:00

'Five minutes, put on your suit or whatever,' the goon barked from halfway up the stairs.

'Tiffany?' Ken asked again, as he flicked on a hallway light, opened his daughter's bedroom door and looked relieved not to find her. Then he shouted back to the goon. 'No sign of my daughter.'

Ken got a surprise as he stepped into the bedroom he shared with his wife. The quilt on the bed had been straightened up and his suit, shirt, tie and briefcase had been spread over it. It was everything he needed for work, but he never laid clothes out on the bed like this.

'Give me your work phone,' the goon said, following Ken into the bedroom.

'I'll need it soon,' Ken said, as he tried to understand who would set his clothes out like this, and why.

The goon grunted. 'Once you get to the town hall, I'll let you have the phone for work calls. But our people will have eyes on you the whole time.'

Ken decided that the deliberate way the suit had been laid on the bed was a message. Whoever sent it not only knew that he'd been kidnapped, but also why he'd been kidnapped and that he would have to return to the house for his suit, phone and briefcase.

*Tiffany must have come home from school, but is she that smart?* Ken wondered as he pulled off his squash shoes and dropped his shorts. He sat on the edge of the bed and his hands trembled as he swapped tennis socks for black work socks.

When Ken reached for the suit trousers, they felt a little heavy and he saw a bulge in the front pocket. Ken tried to hide the bulge as he pulled on the trousers, then he looked over at his minder, who was tapping a message on his phone.

'My guts are turning somersaults,' Ken said, rubbing his belly. 'I have to use the bathroom.'

The goon tutted. 'You just went before we left.'

'Nerves,' Ken said. 'It's not every day you get kidnapped.'

The goon found this funny. 'Can't have you dropping a load in your nice suit, can we?' Don't lock the door. And wipe your face while you're in there. There's blood in your moustache.'

The en-suite was narrow, with the toilet at the far end. Ken's minder had no desire to watch him on the toilet, so he stayed in the bedroom doorway texting. Ken sat on the toilet, then took the mystery object out of his trouser pocket.

It was a small yellow walkie-talkie with a fluorescent pink sticky note stuck to the front. Ken recognised his daughter's tiny, neat handwriting.

> We are listening.
> Turn it on using the knob, then press the
> big button on the side to talk to us.
> P.S. I love you.

Ken reached across to the sink, turned on the mixer tap to make some noise, then held the little radio up to his face.

'Hello?' he whispered.

'Daddy!' Tiffany said anxiously. 'Are you OK?'

'They knocked me around but I'm all right,' Ken said. 'Where are you?'

'Safe,' Tiffany said. 'I watched the video doorbell when I got home from school and I contacted the rebels.'

Ken sounded shocked. 'How do you know rebels, young lady?'

'Daddy, that doesn't matter now. Where are they holding Mummy and Joe?'

'Scary barn place,' Ken said, his voice shaking at the thought. 'It's blacked out inside the van. All I know is, the journey here took twenty minutes. And it must be south of the river, because you know that metal *clunk* you hear when you drive over the middle of the Gala Bridge . . .'

'Did you see the building, or anything else?'

'A barn at the end of a muddy track. I think the door was dark green, and an old truck trailer with no wheels was outside. But there was a really strong smell of pig manure.'

'How do you know it was pigs?' Tiffany asked.

'We camped in a field near pigs when I was in Boy Scouts,' Ken explained. 'It's not a smell you forget.'

'And my friend asks how many of Gisborne's people are inside?'

'There was a big bloke in farm overalls and a woman called Sandra, who's a nasty piece of work. The third guy left in the van with me.'

'Do you think—' Tiffany began, but Ken turned the radio off and pocketed it, because the goon was moving across the bedroom.

'Get a move on!' he ordered, leaning into the bathroom. 'Unless you want my fist in your face again.'

# 26. NOWT ON TELLY

20:03

While Ken spoke to Tiffany on the radio, Flash kept lookout as Robin took a closer look at the van.

The driver's door wasn't locked, but rummaging through the cab was a disappointment: no documents or IDs. Nor was there a satnav that might have contained a list of past trips and favourite destinations.

'Useless,' Robin mumbled to himself as he shut the driver's door quietly and walked back towards the bin store.

Flash pointed out the slightly wonky number plate on the front of the vehicle. 'Check that before you give up.'

Robin shot a cautious glance back towards the house, then crept around the front of the van and gave the crooked number plate a wobble.

'Hello!' he said, when he realised the false plate was held on by two metal clasps, with the van's original registration beneath.

'IMM 403 21,' Robin told Flash. 'Take a photo and send it straight to Marion.'

Robin realised he had horrible-smelling mud all over his hands as he snapped the false plate back onto the clips.

'You wait here until they leave,' Robin told Flash. 'I'm gonna go back to Alan's and try to work out who really owns this van.'

Robin couldn't use the shortcut over the back fence while Ken and his minder were inside, so he had to run to the bottom of the street, go left, run one block then take another left into Alan's street.

By the time Robin arrived, Tiffany had finished speaking to her dad and Marion was sitting at the purple laptop.

'I'll take over,' Robin said confidently. 'No offence, but I'm better at using the Super than you.'

Marion laughed. 'No offence, mighty hacker genius, but I already found where the hostages are.'

'Eh?' Robin gasped.

Marion explained. 'Ken Stalin said he smelled pig manure and it took twenty minutes to drive from there to here. Obviously, I asked the Super to search for pig farms between ten and fifteen kilometres south of Locksley.

'There were eight of those, so I asked the Super who owns them. It gave details for six of the eight farms, including one that is owned by Locksley Holdings. And who do you think owns Locksley Holdings?'

'Guy Gisborne?' Robin guessed.

'Clever boy!' Marion grinned.

'But you didn't get ownership details for all eight farms, so he might own one of the others as well,' Robin noted.

Marion nodded. 'But Flash sent me the photo of the real number plate on the van. When I checked that out, I found it belongs to Cordell David, a known Gisborne associate who lives less than a kilometre from the farm.'

For a final flourish, Marion opened a window on the laptop, bringing up Cordell's photo.

'That's the guy who went in the house with Tiffany's dad,' Robin confirmed.

'You guys are *so* clever,' Tiffany said. 'But this is scary! Are we seriously going to drive to a farm and try to rescue my mum and sister?'

'As soon as my brother gets back here, that's exactly what we're going to do,' Marion said.

Robin tried a joke to calm Tiffany's nerves. 'We might as well, Tiff. If we stay in, there's nothing on telly but boring politics shows.'

# 27. GUNS & YOGA PANTS

20:19

The little Audi was too small for Robin, Marion, Alan, Tiffany, Holly and Flash, so they grabbed the keys for Ken Stalin's seven-seat Range Rover. This would also be better in the mud, and had the advantage that Robin and Marion could sit in the third row of seats and hide their faces.

Two minutes after setting off, a trio of soccer moms were pointing assault rifles at the vehicle, forcing them to halt at a roadblock comprising a Locksley Power Company truck and two builders' skips.

'Hi, Mrs McCafferty,' Tiffany said from the front passenger seat, remembering the woman as the bossy chairperson of a neighbourhood meeting she'd been dragged to years earlier.

'I like how your gun matches your yoga pants,' Flash told the woman, turning on the charm and flicking back his golden hair. 'It's awesome that you're out here protecting our neighbourhood.'

'You need to be super careful,' Mrs McCafferty warned, covering one side of her mouth like she was giving up a prized secret. 'Eastern Way is blocked by fire trucks. Cars diverting through the back streets are being attacked by yobs when they go under the old railway bridge.'

'I'll definitely take the highway,' Flash said. 'Thanks for the advice. You keep safe.'

They drove past two housing blocks and a retirement village. All three had blocked their entrances with cars and bins. They also passed a driving test centre that was being used as a polling station, but nobody was brave enough to come out and vote.

Everyone in the Range Rover who was more than five weeks old gasped when Flash merged onto an elevated highway that gave them a view over central Locksley.

The sheriff's election had made the city tense, and the Brigands had dialled it up by starting a war with Gisborne while his people were busy trying to steal the election. The resulting chaos had drawn hundreds of gang members, petty crooks and bored youths onto the streets looking to smash and steal.

'There's fires everywhere,' Alan said, as he looked into a haze of smoke.

'Three helicopters, untold news drones,' Robin said, gawping. 'Locksley's had riots before, but not this big.'

'Your dad's on, Robin,' Tiffany said, using a button in the armrest to turn up the car radio.

'Mr Hood,' the DJ said. 'There have been dozens of reports of interference at polling stations by both sides and we've had listeners calling this show who say they've witnessed it with their own eyes. Do you deny that your people have been cheating?'

'I've run a clean campaign,' Ardagh answered firmly. 'There may be one or two minor incidents where overenthusiastic supporters have crossed a line. But any unauthorised actions by my supporters are insignificant when compared to the systemic attacks on the electoral process by my opponent, Guy Gisborne.'

Flash laughed as he glanced back at Robin in the driver's mirror. 'Your dad's already learned to lie like a politician.'

Robin squirmed in his seat. 'My dad prides himself on being honest and decent. His head's gonna explode when he finds out what we've been up to. How many fake votes did we print in the end?'

'Sixty thousand,' Marion said, as Holly lay in her lap sucking her fingers. 'But we didn't get all of them into ballot boxes before the streets got too dangerous.'

'There have been reports that your own son, Robin Hood, was involved in an incident involving an explosion in a government building,' the DJ continued. 'And a chase that led to two female police officers being seriously wounded with arrows.'

Robin was pleased to hear that both cops were alive, even if they had been planning to hand him over to Gisborne for the £1 million bounty . . .

'My son does not live with me and I have no knowledge of his actions,' Ardagh said, sounding uncomfortable. 'Robin is wanted for a number of alleged crimes. Since I was recently released from prison on licence, I am not allowed to associate with Robin or any of his associates.'

As the radio interview continued, a deep *boom* made the car's side windows shudder, and a blue flash lit up the street that ran beneath the elevated highway.

'What was that?' Tiffany blurted.

'The road shook,' Flash said. 'I felt that through the steering wheel.'

'Maybe one of those big news drones crashed into a building?' Alan suggested.

'Too loud for that,' Marion said. 'Probably gas exploding in a burning building.'

'Insanity,' Robin gulped, as he shook his head. 'At this rate there'll be nothing left for my dad to be sheriff of.'

The few cars on the highway weren't hanging around, and Flash hit 150 kph as they crossed the Macondo River. He had to go slower on the unlit country road out to the pig farm.

'Good job I screenshotted the map,' Marion said, as branches clattered against the side of the car. 'No phone signal or data out here. Keep your eyes peeled for a dirt track in a few hundred metres.'

They'd lose the element of surprise if the Range Rover came blasting down the farm track. So, after passing the entrance Flash pulled off-road into a tangle of bushes.

'You stay here with Holly,' Flash told Marion. 'If she wakes up there's a bottle of formula in the armrest and nappies in the carrier bag.'

'Why me?' Marion groaned.

'You have a baby sister and those adorable little brothers. I've seen you feed and change nappies like a pro.'

'Whatever,' Marion said sourly. 'To be fair, Robin would probably drop Holly on her head.'

'Where's Holly's mum, anyway?' Alan asked. 'Shouldn't a baby be breastfed at five weeks?'

Flash was usually full of himself, but Alan's comment made him wilt like he'd been slugged in the belly.

'Let's do the hostage rescue now and the child-rearing debate later,' Robin said firmly. 'Phones don't seem to work out here, and we gave one of our two radios to Tiffany's dad, so we're not gonna be able to communicate.'

Flash's brain snapped back into focus. 'Alan, I want you in the driver's seat in case we need to leave in a hurry,' he said. 'I'm leaving the car in drive, so be careful not to hit the accelerator pedal when you get in.'

'I've only ever driven my dad's Mercedes in circles around a car park,' Alan said warily.

Flash shrugged. 'It's an automatic. On a deserted country road, it's easier than driving a quad bike through the forest.'

'If you say so,' Alan replied, as he opened his door to move up front.

'Tiffany, are you sure you're good to go in with Flash?' Robin asked.

'It's *my* family in that barn,' she answered determinedly.

Robin reached between the seats to pass Tiffany a can of pepper spray. 'I ripped this off a cop earlier. If all goes to plan you won't need it, but better safe than sorry.'

'Alrighty, kiddos,' Flash said, swapping his Brigands colours for a green waxed jacket that he'd taken from Alan's house. 'Let's do this.'

# 28. THE BROWN LAGOON

20:52

There wasn't much moonlight as Flash and Tiffany led the way up the muddy track towards the barn, with Robin giving them cover from twenty metres behind.

'This muck stinks,' Flash said, keeping a quiet conversation going because he could see that Tiffany was scared.

'At least you've got boots,' Tiffany said. 'One of the documents the Super pulled up said that Gisborne got fined because the lagoon where all the pig poo ends up keeps overflowing and flooding this land.'

'So, we're ankle-deep in crap and your family's being held hostage,' Flash said, pretending to be cheerful. 'Bet you never expected that when you got out of bed this morning.'

Flash was handsome and charming in a roguish way, and Tiffany almost smiled.

'Holly's beautiful,' Tiffany said.

'Honestly, looking after my tiny girl scares me way more than going into this building. Holly's mum, Agnes, freaked out after she was born and ran off. Says she doesn't want a baby. Told me I could drown Holly in the bath for all she cared.'

'Really? Jesus . . .'

'Hormones, probably,' Flash said, but now they could see the barn and he made a *shush*.

They looked back. Robin gave a thumbs up before taking cover behind the disintegrating truck that Tiffany's dad had described. The moonlight didn't amount to much, but a yellowish glow came from a barred window halfway down the narrow barn.

Flash tapped his side to make sure he could feel his gun under the waxed jacket. There was no bell, so he pounded on the door.

'Hello, hello?'

Tiffany shuddered as she heard boots on a hard floor inside. They were both surprised when a woman – presumably Sandra – stepped out of a door at the side of the building. She was a skinhead, dressed in filthy mustard-coloured dungarees and with tattoos covering most of her gigantic arms.

'What's all this?' Sandra asked grumpily.

She had no idea that Robin Hood was fifteen metres away with his bow aimed at her chest. But unless things went badly wrong, he'd avoid shooting until Tiffany's mum and sister were safe.

'Mike Finch,' Flash lied. 'Cordell said you'd be expecting me.'

'Cordell left an hour ago.'

'This is Tiffany,' Flash explained, as he gave her a two-fingered jab between the shoulder blades. 'I picked her up as she left her pal's house. Cordell said to bring her here to join her mum and brother.'

Flash's story made sense and Sandra relaxed. 'Nobody tells us nothing out here.'

'Phones are down, everyone's busy,' Flash said. 'You should see Locksley. Fires like something out of a movie.'

'Let that dump burn,' Sandra said, eyeballing Tiffany. 'Look at you with your short skirt and Year Nine attitude. You gonna give me trouble?'

'No,' Tiffany said, terrified.

'I made your little brother bawl when he gave me lip,' Sandra said. 'You'll get the same.' She shoved Tiffany into the barn, then looked at Flash. 'Drive safe, pal. I'll take her from here.'

Flash needed to get inside, where he could take out Sandra and the person Ken Stalin had described as a *big bloke* before they had a chance to harm the hostages.

'Before I go, could I use your toilet?' Flash said, giving his best white smile. 'I've been bouncing around all day, running errands for the boss. Maybe a glass of water if it's not too much trouble.'

Sandra seemed immune to Flash's charm, but still gestured for him to step inside.

'Coffee?' Sandra asked. 'It's only instant, but it'll keep you awake.'

'Even better,' Flash said.

As Flash stepped inside, Sandra grabbed a handful of Tiffany's hair and gave her an almighty shove.

'Kneel with hands on your head, brat,' Sandra ordered.

As Sandra pointed Flash towards the toilet, Tiffany realised why her dad got chills when he'd mentioned the barn. The teenager had imagined some random barn with hay bales, but this place was sinister.

Stinking boot prints trailed across the floor. One third of the barn was an open space, with knives and tools hanging on the wall. Hooks and nooses dangled from the ceiling and there was a decaying dentist's chair, fitted with leather straps to hold someone in place.

The rest of the barn was a narrow corridor with four cells built crudely from concrete blocks. As Tiffany tried not to imagine the things that had happened to Guy Gisborne's enemies in this building, the big bloke her dad had described backed out of a cell and clanked its metal door.

'Great, you're putting the kettle on,' the big man said to Sandra. 'I could murder a cuppa and a Scotch egg. Is this the daughter Cordell didn't pick up this morning?'

Sandra nodded. 'Bloke who brought her round is in the toilet. Looks frazzled, so I'm doing him a coffee before he heads back to town.'

As the man walked past Tiffany he swept his rubber-gloved fingers across her face and left a smear of dirt.

'You're right to be scared, Tiffany,' he purred nastily. 'Who's the guy that brought her?'

Tiffany was so scared she thought she was going to vomit as she heard Flash flushing the toilet.

'Mike somebody,' Sandra said, while spooning instant coffee into a mug. 'Young blondie. Boy-band hair and a wispy beard.'

The man shrugged as he peeled off his rubber gloves. 'Gisborne's got so many people now, I can't keep track.'

Flash stepped out of the toilet, and gasped.

He'd instantly recognised the big bloke as a man called Gordon who used to play pool at a biker joint in town. Simultaneously, Gordon recognised the cocky young biker who'd conned him out of £200 by nudging in the black ball with his arm, then getting all his biker pals to back him up and deny that it had happened.

'Flash, ah-ah!' Gordon roared.

'Cut-Throat's boy?' Sandra said, not quite believing it.

Flash reached for the gun beneath his jacket, but Sandra got to the electric kettle faster and flung the near-boiling water in his face. As Flash stumbled backwards, he fired a bullet into the floor.

Tiffany stood up and screamed, 'Robin!'

Sandra leaped on Flash, landing huge punches with one hand while the other tried to take his gun. As they clattered into a little table and knocked a bunch of stuff on the floor, Gordon snatched a big metal claw from the row of implements hanging on the wall.

Tiffany felt like her legs were going to buckle as she stood, reaching for the little can of pepper spray hooked to the waistband of her school skirt.

Flash screamed horribly.

Gordon swung the claw at Tiffany and roared, 'Back on the ground!'

Tiffany ducked the swinging claw, then thrust her arm upwards and blasted pepper spray into Gordon's open mouth. He immediately began to choke, dropping the claw and stumbling sideways into the wall.

Robin had heard the gunshot, but the door was locked from the inside and didn't budge when he tried a shoulder barge.

Tiffany was ruthless, emptying the whole can of pepper spray in Gordon's face. Flash seemed to be barely conscious, but Sandra's massive arms kept pounding him as Tiffany dropped the empty spray can and ran to open the door.

Robin charged in with his bow. At this range an arrow could easily pass clean through Sandra and hit Flash too, so he used the police stun gun and shot her in the arse.

As Sandra spasmed from the shock of eighty thousand volts, Flash pushed her off. Tiffany moved fast, grabbing a shovel off the wall and belting Sandra over the head. There was a highly satisfactory *clang*.

'Mummy!' Tiffany shouted, running desperately towards the cells at the back of the barn.

The first cell smelled horrific and held a barefoot man wearing nothing but badly ripped tracksuit bottoms.

'Tiffany!' a little boy shrieked from the far end.

Robin wasn't sure how long the pepper spray would keep the giant down, so he notched an arrow and shot it through Gordon's wrist, pinning him to the wooden floor.

'You OK?' Robin asked as he turned around to look at Flash.

'I need keys to open the cells,' Tiffany shouted.

Robin wasn't listening, because he was staring in horror. Blood soaked Flash's midriff and a large kitchen knife stuck out from his belly.

# 29. TOUGH ON CRIME

21:09

Guy Gisborne's campaign team and the local branch of the People's Party had hired the ballroom of the Grand Salon Hotel.

Back when Locksley manufactured two million cars a year, the Grand Salon was one of a dozen five-star hotels in the city centre. Now, the city centre's last surviving hotel was run down and the upper floors permanently closed.

But the Grand Salon's ballroom remained a decent venue for a gathering, especially when a small fortune had been spent pimping it up with huge TOUGH ON REBELS, TOUGH ON CRIME banners, slick video projections from Marjorie Kovacevic's presidential campaign and a vast net stuffed with red, white and blue balloons that would – hopefully – drop when victories for Gisborne and Marjorie were announced in a few hours' time.

While rioters rioted, looters looted and fires raged across town, the block of city streets around the Grand Salon was an oasis, protected by dozens of cops and fifty of Gisborne's finest thugs.

Little John felt conspicuous as he arrived in the giant presidential limousine and waited while a powerful motor opened its half-ton blast-proof rear door.

As he got out and straightened his suit jacket, John was surprised there was no press or TV to film his arrival, just a local photographer who was being paid to snap every guest as they arrived to make them feel important.

Clare took John's hand and led the way up a dozen carpeted steps. She'd never been a girly girl, and had chosen shiny punkish boots and a navy pinstripe suit over the shoulderless red dress her mum wanted her to wear.

Officer Scott followed John up the stairs and another who'd scouted the location in advance politely nodded and said, 'Good evening, Mr Kovacevic.'

'It's Mr Hood,' John corrected. 'Better still, call me John.'

There were stares and a little murmur as John and Clare entered the noisy chatter of the ballroom. A curly-haired man John had never seen before slapped him on the back and said, 'Aren't you a big fellow? I think your mother is really going to change this country for the better.'

'Let's hope so,' John said doubtfully, then turned towards Clare and whispered, 'I bloody hate these events.'

Clare flicked up one evil eyebrow. 'We should get drunk.' She grinned.

She chased down a waiter holding a tray of champagne glasses, but the guy knew Clare was the underage daughter of the most dangerous man in town and pointed her towards the soft drinks.

As Clare used a bottle opener on a Rage Cola, John poured a handful of salted nuts down his throat, then almost choked as he saw Guy Gisborne stride towards them.

Gisborne was a squat, powerfully built man who typically sported black jeans and a leather jacket. But for political purposes his hair had been tamed and his wardrobe switched for light grey suits and bright ties to make him look more approachable.

'How's my girl?' Gisborne said, giving Clare a kiss. 'Where's the dress your mum got for you?'

'I'm not five.' Clare snorted. 'She doesn't tell me what to wear.'

Gisborne shrugged, then smiled as he offered John his hand. 'And how's Little John? Did you win your match this afternoon?'

It wasn't easy for John to grin and shake the hand of a man who'd whipped him, thrown his dad in jail and put a million-pound bounty on the head of his little brother. But Gisborne was also his girlfriend's dad, and life was simpler if they acted civil in public.

'We won with a late try,' John said.

'And your dinner?'

'We booked a Japanese place that some girls at Barnsdale raved about,' Clare said. 'But everywhere closed early. We ended up eating mac and cheese with John's Auntie Pauline.'

'Love a bit of comfort food,' Gisborne said, then stepped closer to John and slapped him on the shoulder. 'Can you believe your mum is gonna be the gosh-damned president! When you get down to Capital City, you send her my biggest congratulations. She and I go way back. We were in the same class at school.'

'My dad was in your class too,' John said. 'You were *all* good friends back then.'

Gisborne was clearly irritated by the mention of Ardagh, and Clare tried to smooth things over.

'I bet a million people want to talk to you, Dad. Don't let us waste any more of your time.'

Clare groaned once Gisborne was out of earshot. 'He's so fake,' she complained. 'Kissing your butt because your mum's gonna be president. I can't believe I used to try and copy everything he did.'

'Yeah,' John said, laughing. 'You were basically an idiot until you met me.'

'Now I'm *really* glad I wore these boots,' Clare growled, as she gave her boyfriend a playful kick on the shin.

# 30. BELLY TUBE TANGLE

21:11

Tiffany ran back from the cells towards Gordon, who was retching spit and pepper spray, while groaning in pain from the arrow pinning his wrist to the floor.

Flash gripped the knife sticking out of his belly.

'You'll bleed out if you pull it,' Robin warned.

'It hurts so bad,' Flash said, tears streaking down his cheek.

'We'll get you to a hospital soon.'

Flash shook his head. 'If I go near a hospital, they'll check my ID and the cops will throw me in jail.'

'Better jail than dead,' Robin said, as Tiffany patted down Gordon's overall and found a pocket with keys.

'I can stand,' Flash said, but when he tried to move, he howled and slumped back to the floor.

'I'll get Alan to drive the car up,' Robin said. 'Take deep breaths and hold your stomach to stem the bleeding.'

At the other end of the barn, Tiffany studied Gordon's keychain and found four numbered keys for the cells.

'Don't leave me,' the young lad in cell number three pleaded as Tiffany passed his door.

'I won't,' Tiffany said, sliding a key in the lock of cell number one, which had her mum and brother inside.

Joe shot through the door and squealed as he hugged his big sister.

'That lady kicked me hard,' he said, with all the fury a six-year-old can muster. 'I'm glad you hit her with the shovel.'

'What is all this?' Tiffany's mum asked as she left the cell. 'Is your father safe? What time is it?'

'Nine-ish,' Tiffany said, backing up to release the young man, Joe still clamped to her waist.

The filthy youth cried with relief as his cell door swung open. 'I was sure I'd end up as pig food,' he sobbed.

'How long have you been here?' Tiffany asked, gagging from his body odour.

'Weeks and weeks. Is that Robin Hood?'

Tiffany's mum needed a few seconds to get her head straight after leaving the cell, but once she did, she switched to mum mode and rushed over to Flash.

'Can you help him?' Robin asked desperately. 'I did basic first aid at Sherwood Castle, but this is way beyond me.'

'Have you called an ambulance?' she asked.

Robin shook his head. 'It's too dangerous to stick around waiting for an ambulance, and even if it wasn't, the mobile networks are messed up because there's riots in town.'

Tiffany's mum sighed. 'I haven't worked in healthcare since Tiffany was born, but I trained as a dental nurse. We can bandage him to stop the external bleeding, but there's a whole tangle of tubes and organs in the gut. It'll need a surgeon to pull that knife out safely.'

'Not hospital,' Flash moaned. 'Call Dr Death. She fixes up bikers all the time.'

'Dr Death?' Robin said, wondering if Flash was hallucinating. 'Seriously?'

'Just her nickname,' Flash said. 'Call my dad. He'll know how to get hold of her.'

'We'll try when we get phone signal,' Robin said, then looked around at Tiffany's mum. 'Can you keep an eye while I run down and get our car to pick him up?'

As Robin stood up, Tiffany jangled Gordon's keys in front of him. 'There's a key for a Toyota on here. Did you see any cars parked when you were waiting outside?'

Robin nodded. 'Around the far side.'

Robin took the keys and headed for the door. At the same time, the filthy young prisoner crouched down to search through the unconscious Sandra's overalls.

'If I die, swear you'll look after Holly,' Flash yelled desperately after Robin.

'Nobody's gonna die,' Robin said sternly, but he felt far from sure as he stepped outside.

Halfway around the barn, Robin sank into calf-deep mud that almost sucked off his boot. At the far end there was a concrete paddock, with a battered Toyota pickup and a tiny VW hatchback.

Beyond the paddock a gravel track curved several hundred metres around the edge of a stinking lagoon filled with urine and excrement. This came from a huge metal building on the far side, where thousands of pigs spent their short lives crammed into tiny metal stalls.

As Robin unlocked the Toyota, he noticed two men walking briskly down the path and guessed they'd heard the shot. Then he saw that the aged pickup had a manual gear shift, and Robin didn't know how to drive one.

'Just my luck,' he moaned.

As he backed away from the pickup, Robin saw the former inmate of cell three running through the mud, still barefoot and shirtless. He'd found Sandra's keys and used them to unlock the Volkswagen.

'Can you drive?' Robin asked hopefully. 'I might need your help lifting Flash onto the pickup bed.'

'I'm dead if they catch me again,' the guy said, as he jumped in Sandra's car and started the engine.

'Selfish dick!' Robin gasped as the Volkswagen blasted off.

Adding insult to injury, Robin's hoodie and trousers got pelted with mud as the VW shot across the muddy path towards the road.

'I wish we'd left you in there,' he roared, shaking a fist.

Robin was tempted to shoot out the Volkswagen's rear tyre and teach the youth a lesson, but the two men on the path were a bigger concern. He hurdled a giant puddle as he ran back inside. Tiffany's mum had managed to prop Flash against the wall and was winding a giant reel of duct tape around his wound.

'Can you drive manual?' Robin asked her. 'There's two guys coming our way and probably more of Gisborne's scumbags at the pig farm next door.'

'I'll drive,' Tiffany's mum agreed, then instructed her daughter. 'Take this duct tape and keep winding it around his belly. It needs to be tight, even if he moans. Joe, help Mummy and keep looking for another reel of that tape. But be careful not to touch any sharp things.'

The two men on the path had broken into a run when they saw the Volkswagen speed off. As Robin rushed back outside, he walked right into one of them.

'What are you playing at?' the man demanded, grabbing Robin's hoodie. 'You out here looting? You from the city?'

As Robin twisted loose and went for his bow, the man saw Flash and the bloody mess inside the door.

'Hands up, I will shoot!' Robin shouted.

As the men put their hands up, Robin got his first proper look at them. A slim guy in his twenties and the bald beefy one who'd grabbed him. They were both unarmed and wore matching rubber boots, black trousers and shirts with *Pelham's Pork Products* embroidered on the pocket.

'You work with the pigs?' Robin said, realising they weren't Gisborne goons. 'Why'd you come down here?'

'We heard a bang,' the bald one answered. 'There's a lot of accidents on farms and we thought someone might be hurt.'

'I recognise you,' the younger man added, craning his neck to study the racks of knives and the sinister dentist's chair inside. 'What is this place?'

'Your worst nightmare,' Robin said, as Tiffany's mum stepped outside to join them.

'You look strong,' she told the men, taking charge like a bossy schoolteacher. 'I'm going to need your help lifting my patient onto the back of a truck.'

# 31. SOMEONE'S IN A MOOD

21:45

Clare and John had done their best to avoid everyone. They filled paper plates with chicken wings and cocktail sausages, then hid behind one of the thick marble pillars that supported the ballroom's wrap-around balcony.

There was patriotic classical music, a few kids running up and down stairs playing tag, and the chatter of a couple of hundred guests. This was less than half the number invited, because people were scared to bring their cars into town when everything was kicking off.

'It's my mum,' John told Clare as he pulled his buzzing phone out of his jacket. Then into the phone, 'Mum, hold on. I need to get somewhere quieter.'

Clare looked miffed as John handed her his plate of party food and jogged out of the ballroom onto a patio. It was shiny from drizzle, and a few people stood around smoking.

'Now I can hear. How's it going in Capital City?'

'I'm emotional,' Marjorie said, surprising her son with a high voice and a hint of a sob. 'If I become president, this will be the greatest night of my life. No, the greatest night of *our* lives!'

'Mum, have you been drinking?'

'No,' Marjorie said, laughing. 'I'm not drunk, I'm happy. But I'm also scared. Being president is full-on. I probably won't get a day off for five years. Ten, if I win a second term.'

'Thirty, if you change the constitution and become dictator for life,' John joked.

Marjorie laughed and John felt confused.

His mum was a brutal, ruthless, power-grabbing operator and he agreed with almost none of the things she wanted to do as president. But he was also excited about living at the Presidential Palace, and when he sat with his mum chatting or eating breakfast, she was a thoughtful, lonely person who he kind of liked.

'I've got so much security,' Marjorie said. 'I went to pee and they sent two women with machine guns into the bathroom ahead of me. One poor lass looked like she was going to faint.'

'I've got some close protection too,' John said, as he looked around wondering where they were.

'Have you seen your father today?' Marjorie asked.

'I'm supposed to go to his headquarters when I leave in an hour or so, but the streets are crazy. There's barricades going up everywhere, so I've got no idea if I'll make it.'

'I really just called to say hi while I had a couple of free minutes,' Marjorie told her son. 'My campaign manager Darcy is giving me a look. I've got to change and have my make-up done. What time are you scheduled to arrive in Capital City?'

'I'll leave after my dad's result gets announced, I think,' John said. 'I'd guess 1am to 2am.'

'First night at the Presidential Palace tonight,' Marjorie said. 'Not bad for an awkward foster home kid from Locksley.'

'You haven't won yet,' John reminded her.

'Gotta go, love you,' Marjorie said, then blew a kiss before hanging up.

John decided to take a leak before rejoining Clare in the ballroom. As he found the sign for the men's and turned into a narrow corridor, he passed the half-open door of a wheelchair-accessible toilet.

Two of Gisborne's goons were in there, and Gisborne himself sat on the toilet lid shouting into his mobile phone. It was loud enough for John to hear Gisborne's half of the conversation.

'How hard can it be? All they had to do was look after a woman and her brat for half a day. How could Robin possibly find where we were holding them? And when did this happen?'

There was a pause.

'HALF AN HOUR AGO? Then why am I only hearing this now?'

The thug nearest the doorway saw John going by and hastily shut the door, but Gisborne was raging so hard that it made little difference. And now the door was closed, John could stand in the hallway and listen.

'Get Ken Stalin in a back room and lock ... What? What? I don't care how many rebels are in the town hall,' Gisborne continued. 'If Stalin finds out his family are safe, my whole plan is down the toilet ... Robin Hood, what? I'm sick of hearing the name of that short-arsed, snot-nosed—'

John didn't hear any more because Gisborne had ripped a paper towel dispenser off the wall. There was a big metallic thud as he smashed the dispenser against the sink.

'Out of my way!' Gisborne roared as he stormed past his two goons.

John was right there when Gisborne kicked the toilet door and charged out, but Gisborne seemed not to notice. As John carried on to the men's toilets, Gisborne went the other way, with his goons dropping back, and ranted to himself.

'Robin Hood, Robin Hood, Robin Hood,' Gisborne raged. 'I swear, the next person who says that name in front of me is dead! And when I get hold of him! Oh, when I get hold of him ...'

# 32. LIVE TO MILLIONS

21:49

Alan drove the Range Rover back towards town, cautiously following Tiffany's mum in the Toyota pickup. Flash was sprawled out on the pickup bed, moaning in pain and barely conscious after losing so much blood.

Robin rode in the Range Rover with Marion, Tiffany, Joe and Holly. It felt like a miracle when Marion got two signal bars on her phone and called her dad. By the time they reached the edge of Locksley, Cut-Throat had six bikers waiting for them in the parking lot of a shuttered Mindy Burger.

Two bikers took the pickup and used it to take Flash to Dr Death's underground clinic. Tiffany's mum took over from Alan behind the wheel of the Range Rover, and four heavily armed bikers formed an escort as they drove past smashed windows, looted shops and hundreds of burnt and burning cars.

Robin was in the third row of seats, with Tiffany's brother Joe wriggling on his lap, and every window open because the aroma of stinking clothes and boots was mingling with Holly's dirty nappy.

'I just changed her.' Marion sighed.

'And it was green!' Alan said.

Tiffany's mum was stressed out, but managed to laugh. 'It's often green when they're first born.'

As the biker escort led them around a barricade that had been set ablaze with petrol bombs, their convoy was joined by two cars containing well-armed rebel security officers.

'They're not taking any chances,' Robin said, then Marion shushed him.

'It's the exit poll, finally!' Marion said, as Tiffany turned up the radio.

'The News 24 exit poll asks people who they voted for as they leave hundreds of polling stations around the country. Historically, exit polling is an accurate indicator of the actual election result, which we will get in a few hours' time when all the votes around the country have been counted.

'Normally, this poll is released the moment polling stations close at 9.30pm, but tonight's results have been delayed because of disturbances in Locksley and several other places around the country. But we do now have a final exit poll and—'

The radio presenter paused for dramatic effect.

'The poll predicts a victory for Marjorie Kovacevic in the presidential race, with fifty-seven per cent of the votes. That is a better result for Marjorie than most pre-election polls suggested, and it goes to show that the former Sheriff of Nottingham has done a spectacular job of turning her campaign around over the final weeks of the campaign.'

Marion and Alan groaned loudly.

'People are so dumb,' Robin growled, kicking the seat in front of him.

'We're screwed,' Alan said. 'If Marjorie sends in tanks to clear rebels and migrants out of Sherwood, there's no way we can beat them.'

'Will she, though?' Tiffany asked. 'Politicians never do half the stuff they promise.'

Now the presenter started talking about local results. 'While it looks like Mo Haim will serve a second term as mayor of Capital City, violence in and around Locksley has brought national attention to who will be the next Sheriff of Nottingham.

'Unfortunately, our exit poll has nothing to say on the battle between Guy Gisborne and Ardagh Hood. Staff on the ground in Locksley were forced to withdraw after several violent incidents. And with many reports of fraud and corruption by supporters on both sides, it seems increasingly likely that the race to become the new sheriff may end up being decided in the courts.'

The Range Rover and its escorts slowed as they drove into Locksley's Central Square, passing the city's main court building and abandoned art gallery. Across the square, an office building used by Guy Gisborne still smouldered after being attacked by Brigands earlier in the day.

The front of the town hall was being protected by a line of cops. There were three TV news trucks behind the line, though one had been trashed and tipped on its side when rioters briefly broke through police lines.

Rather than confront the cops, the rebel convoy came to a screeching halt by a side entrance where a supporter was waiting to let them in. Robin, Marion, Alan, Holly, Joe, Tiffany, Tiffany's mum and their phalanx of bikers and rebel guards charged in and shut the door behind them before the cops out front knew what was happening.

The group were led through to a grim, low-ceilinged hall. Vote counting had just started, and ballot boxes from all over the county were being wheeled in at the back. Boxes were opened, then the votes inside were distributed among more than a hundred tables. Each vote was checked by workers, who then entered the results into clattering grey counting machines that looked like old-fashioned typewriters.

Gisborne for sheriff was registered by pressing S2, a vote for Marjorie P1, and so on. At the end, the voting papers were put back in the black boxes in case someone protested the result and wanted the votes counted again.

While the count seemed orderly, the public area beyond it frothed with anxious candidates, campaign staff, press,

TV crews, cops, rebels, thuggish Gisborne supporters and even a few rioters who'd breached security and were spraying graffiti on walls and ceiling tiles.

As Tiffany's family and their escorts jogged into this space, a bunch of Gisborne supporters lined up to confront them. Robin and Marion stayed back near the side entrance, hoping not to be recognised.

While rebels and Gisborne supporters traded punches, kicks and spit, Ken Stalin spotted his wife and children. He ran between the lines of people counting votes, while rebel security chief Azeem and her sister Lyla walked behind to stop any of Gisborne's people getting at him.

The TV crews and journalists knew nothing about the Stalin family kidnapping, but they realised that something big was happening and moved as close as they dared, filming the scuffles and desperate to speak to someone who knew what was going on.

The four cops in the room decided to stay out of it, while several bikers charged in because they enjoyed a good scrap, especially if they could steal a couple of phones or a photographer's expensive camera while they were at it.

'I'm not sure what's going on here,' a TV journalist told his camera. 'This is News 24, broadcasting live from the count room at Locksley town hall, amidst scenes of utter chaos.'

Press cameras flashed as one of Gisborne's people picked up a chair and tried to hit Ken Stalin with it. Lyla blasted the chair thrower with a stun gun, though the chair caught her painfully on the elbow.

Seconds later, six-year-old Joe made it between all the grown-up legs and yelled, 'Daddy,' as he grabbed his father. A tiny camera drone clipped Tiffany's head as she joined them. Her mum broke down in uncontrollable sobs as she watched her kids hugging their dad.

While the Stalins reunited, the News 24 camera operator backed into one of the tables being used to count votes and got barked at by a bossy election official.

'Stay clear of the counting area!' he demanded.

As the camera operator spun around, she noticed two teenagers standing at the back of the rebel group.

'Jenny, where are you going?' the TV reporter shouted. But then the reporter saw them too and his head practically exploded.

'This is unbelievable!' the reporter gushed importantly. 'I am now in the count room at Locksley town hall and standing in front of me are two wanted fugitives, Robin Hood, who needs no introduction, and Marion Maid, who recently escaped from Pelican Island prison.

'Robin, you are live in front of millions of viewers watching *Election Night Special*. We've seen chaotic scenes and some sort of reunion. Have you any idea what is going on?'

The TV journalist gulped air as he got close because Robin's trousers were covered in vile-smelling mud.

'I'll tell you what happened,' Robin blasted, proudly holding up his bow. 'Guy Gisborne kidnapped the family of returning officer Ken Stalin. Gisborne said that he would kill Stalin's family if he didn't fix this election.

'But we rescued them and Gisborne failed. Just like our new president will fail if she sends the army into Sherwood Forest and tries to kill hundreds of innocent people.'

The journalist pointed his microphone at Marion. 'You're holding a baby – is that yours?'

'Of course it's not mine, you knobhead,' Marion spat. 'I'm thirteen.'

Robin cracked up laughing because Marion had called someone a knobhead on live TV, but more journalists had spotted them. There was only a thin line of rebel security and bikers protecting Robin and Marion from an aggressive crowd of Gisborne supporters, and the cops were also starting to take an interest.

'What about the vote-rigging incident at Freud Park earlier?' the TV reporter asked Robin. 'Do you deny being involved in a rebel plot to stuff ballot boxes for—'

Before Robin could answer, Azeem stuck her hand in front of the camera.

'Interview terminated!' she shouted. 'Camera off, unless you want a nip from my stun gun!'

At the same time, Lyla growled at Robin and Marion. 'Are you two completely braindead?' she asked furiously. 'Why come in here instead of asking someone to take you somewhere safe? And my God, Robin, what do you smell like?'

'Mostly pig crap,' Robin said.

'We just followed everyone else,' Marion admitted guiltily.

Azeem realised the TV camera hadn't stopped filming and batted it away.

'Come on,' Lyla said as she led Robin and Marion back towards the side entrance at a run. 'Before you two numpties earn all of us a one-way trip to Pelican Island.'

# 33. BORROWED PANTS

23:01

Azeem got a rebel officer to drive Robin and Marion to the White House. Twenty minutes after arriving, Robin had drunk a cup of tea, cleaned the mud off his filthy boots and taken a shower.

There was a massive bang outside as he towelled off, then quickly dressed in a pair of borrowed jogging pants and a *Vote Ardagh* campaign T-shirt that went down to his knees.

'What was that bang?' asked Robin, stepping into a bedroom where Marion was staring out of a window.

'It's mental out there,' she replied edgily. 'There's heaps of people at the main gate and yobs climbing over the wall.'

'Where's Holly?' Robin asked as he extracted his phone and wallet from his muddy trousers.

'One of the campaign volunteers is taking care of her for a bit. My dad called while you were showering. He's found a number for Agnes.'

'Your dad knows Agnes?' Robin asked.

'Not personally,' Marion explained. 'But Agnes was a member of the Sherwood Women's Union before Marjorie's security team wiped them out, and the Brigands used to supply SWU with fuel and weapons.'

'Now I remember.' Robin nodded. 'That's how Flash met Agnes. But you have to feel sorry for Holly. Two teenaged parents. Raving madman like Flash for a dad, and psycho Agnes McIntyre for a mum.'

'Poor kid's not gonna have it easy,' Marion agreed. 'But at the end of the day Agnes *is* Holly's mum, so I called her and left a message saying we've got her.'

There was a bunch of screams and shouting outside. When Robin and Marion looked out, they saw about twenty random people trying to force their way in the front gate. A rebel security person had knocked them back by electrifying the metal bars with their stun gun.

'Where did all these rioters come from?' Robin asked. 'We're nowhere near the town centre.'

'Mystery,' Marion answered. 'I might go down to the kitchen and see if there's any food left. You coming?'

'I'll catch you up,' Robin said. 'Someone said my dad was here when we arrived. He'll be busy, but I'll try to say hi.'

Robin went into the bathroom to get his boots, but they were still dripping wet. He'd stuffed flannels inside to help them dry out. Since he was only heading down the hall, he decided to go barefoot.

As he followed Marion out of the bedroom, they heard more banging and shouting outside. When they got a view over the banister down to the home's main lobby, they saw campaign volunteers charging around, stuffing documents into black bags and carrying IT equipment to a van parked in front of the house.

'Looks like we're evacuating,' Marion said, sounding curious.

As she headed downstairs seeking food, Robin walked further down the hallway to Will and Emma Scarlock's office. The door was open and a volunteer was scooping stuff from a desk into a big cardboard box.

Will and Ardagh sat by the mantelpiece, having a furious conversation.

'Today has been a disaster,' Ardagh told Will, with uncharacteristic anger. 'I discovered that my own campaign team was printing thousands of fake ballot papers during a live phone-in on Radio Sherwood.'

'I stand by my decision,' Will said resolutely. 'This election is not just about you, Ardagh. It's about protecting the people of Locksley and Sherwood Forest from being ruled by a vicious gangster.'

'I've lost before I've even begun.' Ardagh sighed. 'After today, everyone will say *Ardagh Hood is as crooked as all the other politicians.* And let's face it, they're not wrong.'

'Hey, guys!' Robin interrupted, trying to sound more cheerful and less knackered than he felt.

Will smiled, but Ardagh gave Robin the same look as when he accidentally shot an arrow through the fridge door.

'Did you hear the latest on Flash?' Will asked, grateful for a distraction from his argument with Ardagh.

'Good news?' Robin asked.

'Afraid not. The doctor who fixes up wounded bikers said Flash needed a full surgical team and twenty units of blood to get that knife out safely. The bikers dropped Flash outside Locksley General and cops cuffed him to the hospital bed before he went into surgery.'

'That sucks,' Robin said. 'Did I hear that Neo and Ten Man got busted too?'

'Luckily they got busted at a rural two-man police station,' Will said. 'Tybalt drove up there and made a generous donation to get them released.'

Robin half-smiled. 'I guess there's *some* advantages to our cops being corrupt.'

Ardagh gave a disapproving snort, but before he could say anything, Security Chief Azeem's voice came out of Will's walkie-talkie.

'Two things, boss,' Azeem said. 'I'm still in the count room at Locksley town hall, making sure Gisborne's people can't get near Ken Stalin. He says the count is almost finished and it looks like they'll be ready to announce a new sheriff in thirty to forty minutes.'

'The car is ready, so I'll get Ardagh on the road ASAP,' Will answered.

'Second thing, we've worked out why so many people are turning up at the White House. Gisborne's got people on the street handing £50 to anyone who agrees to head your way and make trouble.'

'Thanks for the intel, Azeem,' Will said. 'We're not going to fight it. Our security teams are exhausted, and why put lives at risk defending our campaign headquarters when the campaign is over? We're clearing out computers and shredding sensitive documents. I sent most of the volunteers home when polling closed. Emma is arranging transport for the rest of us.'

'Very sensible,' Azeem responded.

'I'll see you at the town hall shortly,' Will told her, then pocketed his radio and looked at Ardagh. 'Time to get you on the road.'

'What about me?' Robin asked as the two men stood up.

'We have a good supply of quads and motorbikes,' Will said. 'You, Marion and Alan can head back to Sherwood Castle. There's going to be thirty or forty people heading back that way in the next hour. If everyone rides in well-armed groups, you should be safe from bandits.'

'Makes sense,' Robin agreed, then looked at Ardagh. 'Fingers crossed for the result, Dad.'

Ardagh still looked unhappy as he put a hand on Robin's shoulder and gave it a gentle squeeze.

'I know your heart is in the right place,' Ardagh told Robin softly. 'But you need to put more thought into the things you do, rather than blindly following others.'

# 34. ADULTS BE CRAZY

23:11

Marion went downstairs hoping for a cheese-and-tomato toastie but found a kitchen in chaos. A missile thrown by a rioter had shattered the window over the sink, and a caterer called Anne was frantically packing plates, cutlery and giant saucepans into cardboard boxes.

'Extra hands, please!' Anne pleaded as she handed Marion a twelve-slice commercial toaster. 'This equipment is my livelihood. I need everything loaded in my van out back.'

As Marion waddled outside with the giant toaster, the noise gave her a full sense of the battle going on around them.

Rebel security was comfortably holding the White House's main gate, but the meandering garden wall around the property ran almost two kilometres. There wasn't enough security to defend the perimeter, and any modestly fit person could climb over by standing on a wheelie bin or a pal's shoulders.

Most of the troublemakers who'd made it inside seemed content to trash the greenhouses and outdoor pool area, but a few were carrying big stones from the rock garden and running up to the house to lob them at windows.

'They're not gonna hold out long if Gisborne's sending more people,' Marion told Anne, then stepped back inside and took a box of rattling kitchen implements from the countertop.

As Marion shoved the box in Anne's van, a petrol bomb blast made her jump. Then she saw that a couple of young hooligans had found a ride-on mower and decided to drive it through the flowerbeds.

'Marion?' Robin asked, as he entered the kitchen.

'What's up with you?' Marion asked when she got inside and saw his expression.

'Can you two handle my microwave?' Anne asked.

Robin explained about the argument and Will's plan to evacuate as he and Marion carried the big commercial microwave out to Anne's van. He was so riled up that he forgot he was barefoot until he stepped onto the damp gravel outside.

'As my dad's leaving he goes, *Robin, you should put more thought into things, instead of following others*. But when Dad said it, he was scowling at Will. And Will gave my dad this look, like he wanted to thump him.

'I was so angry with Dad. His campaign would have gone nowhere if Emma and Will hadn't helped. Rebel security have been protecting Dad all day, then he sits there being all high and mighty and having a go at us.'

'Your dad has strong principles,' Marion said as they lowered the big microwave into the back of the caterer's van. 'And you should have figured it out by now: all adults are crazy. I mean, I love my dad, but he's had kids by at least nine women, he's always broke, he gets in stupid fights all the time, and when he's in a mood he ignores my calls and messages for weeks on end.'

Robin nodded. 'At least I'm not Little John.'

Marion laughed. 'Now that *is* complicated.'

They paused to watch as a big BMW sped towards the main gate with Ardagh in the back. Jeers erupted and missiles pelted the car as it exited, followed by two more cars containing Will Scarlock and a crew of rebel security guards.

Marion's phone rang as they got back inside the kitchen.

'Agnes, thanks for calling back,' Marion said, putting the phone on speaker so Robin could hear too.

'I heard they had to take Flash to a real hospital.' Agnes sighed. 'We're wanted for a string of robberies, so you might not see him for a while.'

'I suppose prison's better than dead.' Marion sighed too. 'Like I said in my message, we've got Holly here, safe and well. But Flash said that you got really upset after she was born.'

'I'm embarrassed about how I reacted, Marion,' Agnes said seriously. 'I was in the clinic, holding this tiny scary little human that might die if I didn't look after it properly. I freaked out. Bought a big bottle of vodka, ran to the station and drank myself stupid on the first train that turned up.'

'Don't beat yourself up,' Marion said sympathetically. 'Everyone's exhausted after giving birth. Every time one of my mums has a baby, the hormones make her emotional for weeks.'

'Let's arrange a meet so I can get Holly,' Agnes said. 'I'm ready to be a mum now.'

'One of the campaign volunteers has her right now,' Marion explained. 'We're at Ardagh Hood's campaign headquarters in north Locksley, but there's rioters everywhere and we're about to abandon ship. If you can get to Sherwood Castle, you can pick Holly up there.'

'If you're alone, you should wait until tomorrow when it's light,' Robin added.

'Robin?' Agnes asked. 'Is that Robin?'

'I'm pretty sure that's who I am,' Robin agreed.

'I know you're not my biggest fan,' Agnes told him. 'I *really* appreciate you helping me. But with the stuff that's gone down between me and the rebels over the years, they're not exactly gonna put out the welcome mat at Sherwood Castle.'

Robin laughed. 'True.'

'I've been staying at a friend's place in north Locksley,' Agnes said. 'I'd really like to get Holly tonight. I can't stop thinking about her. I guess my maternal instinct is kicking in.'

'We'll be heading towards Sherwood Castle in—' Marion began.

Then there was another huge bang. This one made the whole house shake and set off a deafening fire alarm.

'What was that?' Agnes asked.

'No idea,' Marion said, holding the phone close to her face so she could hear over the alarm.

'There's an abandoned pub,' Agnes said.

'What?' Marion shouted.

'A pub. If you're heading to Sherwood Castle, it will only add five minutes to your journey. I can pick Holly up there.'

'I can barely hear over this alarm!' Marion shouted. 'Can you message me the location?'

'I can't hear you over the alarm,' Agnes shouted back. 'I'll text you.'

As Marion ended her call and started tapping out a message, Emma Scarlock was running down the main staircase into the adjoining entrance hall.

'Everybody out! Fire! Evacuate now and assemble out back.'

Robin ran into the hallway and stopped in front of Emma. 'What's happening?' he shouted over the screaming alarm.

'Troublemaker got inside, splashed petrol along the second-floor hallway and sparked it,' Emma explained. 'Azeem thinks Gisborne has a double-decker bus full of yobs, coming here to cause even more trouble.'

'Perfect.' Robin sighed.

As Emma ran off to check that all the downstairs rooms were empty, Marion joined Robin in the hall, looking horrified. 'Holly was sleeping upstairs. Did anyone bring her down?'

Robin looked up the staircase. Smoke was billowing from the upstairs hallway and the paint on the double-height ceiling was blistering from intense heat in the rooms above.

'Has anyone seen baby Holly?' Marion shouted, then coughed from a waft of smoke.

Robin glanced around. Pretty much everyone had been on the ground floor, getting ready to leave. He got a chill as he realised they were practically the last people left in the building. Marion moved towards the staircase, but Robin grabbed her arm.

'If Holly's up there, she's dead,' he said bluntly, then remembered that his boots, bow and backpack were upstairs too.

The nearest exit was through the kitchen. Anne the caterer had returned one last time to get her handbag and car keys, and the three of them exited together. The lawns and gravel paths around the house were tinted orange from the flames in the house, and most rioters had backed off, intimidated by the fire and the automatic weapons carried by rebel security.

'Baby Holly!' Marion screamed, as she sprinted to the assembly point at the back of the building. 'Does anyone have Holly?'

A woman in a *Vote Ardagh* T-shirt stopped Robin. 'I grabbed your bow and backpack on my way out.'

'Lifesaver,' Robin told her gratefully, taking his stuff before chasing after Marion.

'Holly!'

Three mini-convoys of motorbikes and quad bikes had been preparing to depart when the blaze started on the upper floor. Robin found himself standing at the rear of the burning house, smoke tickling his throat, while gear was loaded onto trailers and noisy two-stroke bike engines spluttered to life.

'I've got her,' a rebel security officer called Grant said.

When Robin caught up with Marion, he had his pack and bow but still nothing on his feet. His best friend was doubled over, crying with relief.

'Is she yours?' Grant asked, as he passed Holly over.

Marion hugged Holly tight. 'I've never been so scared,' she told Robin. Then she scowled at the stocky rebel officer. 'Grant, you were at my Welcome Home party after I escaped. Did I look eight months pregnant?'

'Sorry, Marion.' Grant laughed. 'I've been on my feet since six this morning and my brain is fried. Besides, Holly really does look like you.'

Robin hadn't put much thought into this, but he studied Holly's big blue eyes and the shape of her face, then smiled. 'She really does look like you.'

'Everyone needs to get on the bikes and start moving out,' Emma was shouting.

Marion still had tears in her eyes as Holly wrapped a tiny fist around her little finger. 'I really hope Agnes is the mummy you deserve,' she said sadly.

# 35. DISORDERLY DEPARTURE

23:30

Emma Scarlock had organised a departure from the White House, with three convoys comprising eight to ten bikes and quads, each led by someone expert in navigating Sherwood Forest at night and with two armed security officers for protection.

But the plan disintegrated in the face of the huge fire, the threat of attack from rioters, and the fact that many of the campaign volunteers wanted to drive out of the front gate, rather than risk leaving their cars behind to get trashed.

'Please, stick together,' Emma shouted desperately. 'If we panic, we might leave someone behind.'

The first quads were already blasting off towards the property's rear gate as Robin and Marion found a pair of dirt bikes. While Marion wrapped the Velcro straps of Holly's crib around her handlebars, Anne the caterer was blasting her horn, trying to get the last two guards holding the front gate to open up and let her out.

The fire had also attracted the attention of a buzzing news drone.

'This is chaos – I'm not sticking around,' Marion said.

Robin's bare foot hurt as he kick-started his bike. He'd trodden on something sharp, but he didn't have enough time or light to check it out. Marion shot off, tailed by Lyla and Grant on a quad bike. But when Robin twisted his throttle, the handlebars wobbled and he almost fell off.

He made a second attempt, rolling a few metres, but he had to jerk the handlebars violently just to go straight. Marion was getting further away and Robin had a horrible sense that he'd get left behind as three more quads shot off in a line.

Robin jumped off the bike and used the light on his phone to look at the front end. It only took a second to find a split in the front tyre big enough to make the whole thing separate from the wheel rim as soon as he'd moved.

'Hey, stop!' Robin shouted, waving his arms as yet another bike skimmed by.

He knew his way to Sherwood Castle, but even if he got through all the rioters, it would be no fun trekking alone in the dark with bare feet.

Luckily, Marion had seen he was missing and had turned back, while Lyla and Grant tailed her on a quad.

'What's up, Doc?' Marion asked, her headlamps blazing in Robin's face.

'Front tyre's wrecked.'

'Climb aboard.'

Robin straddled Marion's bike and locked his arms around her waist.

The rioters were getting bolder now that most of the rebels had driven off. Some lobbed rocks at the windows of the burning house, while two rival gangs had spotted each other and begun a massive, brutal scrap among themselves.

Marion didn't fancy trying to weave through the hordes in the dark. She looked towards the front gate, which was clear now the last two guards had escaped and the crowd had stormed inside.

'I'm going that way,' Marion shouted back to Lyla and Grant on the quad bike.

A couple of rioters dived out of the way as Marion blazed through the front gate, with Robin holding on and Lyla and Grant behind. As she picked up speed they passed another huge house, with rioters climbing over the wall.

'The forest gives us better cover,' Marion shouted back to Robin. 'But we're already on the road and this route gets us to Sherwood Castle quicker.'

'Makes sense,' Robin agreed.

As Marion swept around a corner, she saw the caterer's van they'd helped to pack at the side of the road. There was no sign of anyone, but every window was shattered. The kitchen equipment had been pulled out of the van and smashed up, while others had enjoyed themselves hurling boxes of glassware and frisbeeing plates along the road.

'Scumbags!' Marion gasped as she pulled up.

Lyla and Grant stopped and readied their automatic rifles.

'Anne?' Marion shouted, beginning to search.

Robin thought he heard something on the other side of the road. He crossed carefully, trying to keep his bare feet out of the smashed china and glass. He flinched when he saw Anne, slumped in a ditch, with ripped clothes and one side of her face badly swollen.

'Found her,' Robin shouted, then squatted down. 'Anne, are you awake?'

Anne turned her head and moaned as Robin helped her to sit against the side of the boggy ditch.

'They were like wild animals,' Anne sobbed as Marion, Grant and Lyla joined them. 'I had to stop because they blocked the road. They dragged me out, kicked and punched me, and smashed everything for no reason.'

'I think her arm's broken,' Marion said.

'Anne, do you have a citizenship card?' Grant asked.

'Born and bred, Locksley taxpayer,' Anne said.

Grant looked at Lyla. 'She's eligible for government healthcare, so let's lay her over the back of the quad bike and drop her at Locksley General.'

'What about these two?' Lyla said, pointing to Robin and Marion. 'Emma told us not to let them out of our sight until they're back at Sherwood Castle.'

'We can handle ourselves,' Robin said.

'They could ride to hospital with us, then we'll go to the castle,' Grant suggested.

Robin shook his head. 'Can you imagine how busy it's gonna be at the hospital after a riot? And I'll be on a bike with a bow on my back, so everyone will recognise me.'

'It's only a ten-minute ride from here to the pub where we're meeting Agnes,' Marion said. 'Then I can cut through the forest to the castle. I've done it a hundred times.'

Grant nodded. 'I certainly don't want to leave Holly's mum waiting in the dark, alone in the middle of nowhere.'

Lyla sighed. 'I guess splitting up is the least bad option,' she said. 'Robin has his bow, but what about you, Marion?'

Marion shook her head. 'I had pepper spray and a machine gun, but my stuff was all upstairs when the fire started.'

'Take this,' Lyla said, undoing her holster belt and handing Marion an automatic pistol. 'You know how to use it?'

Marion nodded.

'And don't let your guard down,' Grant warned. 'There's a lot of dangerous people out there.'

# 36. UNPRECEDENTED VOTER TURNOUT

23:41

Little John had said goodnight to Clare and was about to leave the Grand Salon in the presidential limo when he got a message from Ardagh.

> White House under attack and being abandoned.
> Sherriff result announced soon.
> Can we meet at Locksley town hall instead?

Anyone with the surname of Gisborne would have made an awkward guest at Ardagh's headquarters, but the count room was a neutral space. John called Clare, told her about the change of venue, and she agreed to join him for the three-minute drive to Locksley town hall.

'Streets seem quieter,' John noted as he peered through the limo's thick glass.

Scott, the protection officer up front, gave an explanation without being asked. 'Rioting nearly always dies off after a few hours. Looters have to carry stuff home. People get tired, scared or hurt. They need food, or a toilet.'

Scott drove the tank-like limo down a ramp at the back of the town hall and parked at the rear of the count room, where the ballot boxes had been delivered earlier. A second car with two more protection officers pulled up behind as Scott led John and Clare into the counting area.

'Remember what Commander Thrush explained earlier,' Scott said. 'Close protection is difficult in crowded spaces. We can stand close and give you full protection, or stand off to allow you privacy with your father.'

'You can back off,' John said, thinking how weird it would be to have a cop standing next to him. 'I've lived in Locksley my whole life and nobody's killed me yet.'

Most staff had finished counting votes and sat at their tables playing with their phones and hoping they'd be sent home soon. At the centre of the counting area, Ken Stalin stood with a small team checking and rechecking the final count before his big announcement.

The scene in the public part of the hall was as rowdy as earlier, but had split into three distinct groups. The media lined up in front of a little temporary stage amidst tangled cables, camera tripods and microphone stands.

Rebels, bikers and other Ardagh supporters stood around on one side of the room, then there was no man's land down the centre, with a smaller group of Gisborne supporters opposite.

'Evening, Dad,' John said fondly, after spotting Ardagh hidden among taller people. 'This is my girlfriend, Clare.'

'Pleasure to finally meet you, Clare,' Ardagh said. 'Is your father planning to show his face for the result?'

'I don't know my dad's movements,' Clare said, slightly irritated.

'Gisborne better hurry up if he is,' John said, as someone switched on a microphone up on stage and sent a squeal of feedback through the hall's PA system. 'Looks like we barely made it in time.'

At the front of the room, TV reporters touched up their hair and bright rectangular lights lit their faces as every channel covering the election switched to the live coverage.

The line between Gisborne and Hood supporters broke down as people surged towards the stage. Alongside the little platform, Ken Stalin was buttoning his jacket while a young woman brushed lint off his back.

Ken looked drained as he walked up to the microphone. John found himself holding Clare's hand, close enough to the stage to overhear one of the live TV broadcasts.

'This is Oluchi Chanara, live at Locksley town hall. Despite multiple allegations of fraud and vote-rigging by both sides, we are now expecting to hear the result in a sheriff's election that the polls said was too close to call.'

Shouts and jeers from the crowd tailed off as Ken Stalin cleared his throat and began to speak. 'I, Kenneth Derrick Stalin, duly appointed returning officer, hereby declare the result in the election for the office of Sheriff of Nottingham and Warden of Sherwood Forest. The votes were cast as follows:

'Guy Montague Sebastian Gisborne, People's Party candidate, four hundred and eighty-one thousand, seven hundred and sixty-two votes.'

'Beat that!' a Gisborne supporter shouted, as the rest of them cheered and clapped.

John squeezed Clare's hand tight and held his breath as the room quietened down enough for Ken to resume speaking.

'Ardagh Capulet Hood, independent candidate. Five hundred and—'

Ardagh's supporters erupted as soon as they heard the first number.

'Dad did it!' John screamed, letting Clare go as he rushed towards his dad, sending a photographer flying. 'You bloody did it.'

When the noise died off, Ken finally read the rest of the number. 'Five hundred and one thousand, two hundred and eighty-two votes. I hereby declare that Ardagh Capulet Hood is the duly elected Sheriff of Nottingham and Warden of Sherwood Forest.'

'You're a dead man, Stalin!' a burly Gisborne supporter roared as Ken backed away from the lectern. 'Your family too.'

Another Gisborne supporter threw a plastic chair into the crowd of reporters. As Ken backed up, an egg splattered on the back of his jacket.

Across the room there were wild chants of 'Ardagh, Ardagh,' as Little John lifted his father onto his shoulders, almost bashing his head on the low ceiling. As a line of rebels and bikers stepped in to protect Ken Stalin from threats and missiles, TV reporter Oluchi Chanara pushed towards Ardagh, pursued by her camera operator.

'I'm live with Channel 9's election night coverage,' Oluchi said as she reached way up to put her microphone in front of Ardagh. 'How does it feel to be the new Sheriff of Nottingham?'

'Fantastic, fantastic!' Ardagh said, swaying on his son's shoulders as a happy tear dripped off his cheek. 'Nobody thought we could do this. This job is not going to be easy, but the one thing I promise everyone who voted for me is that I'll be in the sheriff's office every day, working hard to make people's lives better.'

Oluchi nodded and a deafening cheer erupted. By the time it subsided, she'd thought of a tougher question.

'Sheriff Hood, around eight hundred thousand adults were eligible to vote in this election. But it seems that you and Guy Gisborne polled almost one million votes. Does that not cast a shadow over this result?'

'I led a clean campaign and am confident that this result will stand,' Ardagh said, wobbling as John tripped. 'If my opponent wishes to dispute the result, he has forty-eight hours in which to lodge a complaint with the Electoral Conduct Authority.'

Oluchi turned towards her camera operator as John put his father down. 'Extraordinary scenes here at Locksley town hall,' she said, speaking to camera. 'Ardagh Hood is celebrating an astonishing underdog victory. But with so many allegations of corruption, you have to wonder if this result will stand. Now I'll hand you back to Lynn Hoapili to get the reaction from our pundits in the Capital City studio.'

# 37. ONE NIGHT AT THE MARQUEE

23:50

The Marquee had been a legendary local music venue – the kind of place where massive bands played to twenty people before they got famous. Now it was a graffitied shell with a caved-in roof, not much different to a thousand other places that had gone under when Locksley's economy tanked.

Marion and Robin took standard precautions as they arrived: shutting off the bike engine, walking the last half-kilometre and checking the dilapidated building from all sides.

Agnes cut a sad, lonely figure, sitting on the hood of a battered beige estate car. A sawn-off shotgun hung from her belt, but that was a standard precaution for a woman on the edge of Sherwood Forest at midnight.

'Stay back and cover me,' Marion whispered.

Robin had been betrayed by Agnes before, so was glad that Marion had chosen to be cautious.

'We should have waited till tomorrow, in daylight,' Robin said as he remembered his dad's advice from earlier: *put more thought into things instead of blindly following others.*

'I'd have preferred it if Grant and Lyla were still with us,' Marion said. 'But we're here now.'

'We could still back out,' Robin whispered. 'Call Agnes. Say we couldn't get here because of the riots.'

But Holly made the decision for them with a sudden squeal. Marion hurried to lift Holly out of the crib, but Agnes had heard.

'Is that you?' Agnes said, raising her arms and moving away from the car.

There wasn't much light, but what Marion could see of Agnes was pitiful. Tatty old trainers, severe acne and scared-looking.

'It's just me,' Marion said, stepping out of cover. 'I've got Holly.'

Agnes dabbed one eye with a fingertip. Marion felt sorry for her and felt her own tears well up because, if Flash was in jail, Agnes was unlikely to stick around. Which meant she might never see her tiny niece again.

'Maybe my family can help,' Marion said as she rested Holly's crib on the hood of the car. 'Money, babysitting. Being a single mum is hard.'

'For sure,' Agnes said, but she didn't sound keen.

Robin was still in the bushes when he heard shuffling behind him. He swung around with his bow, but before he could fire something hit him in the arse. It stung horribly and his thoughts seemed to freeze.

Marion didn't hear the ambush, but she did see one of Robin's arrows launching horizontally into the canopy of trees. When she looked back, Agnes had the shotgun pointing in her face.

'You,' Marion growled as she ducked and butted Agnes in the stomach.

Agnes stumbled back and hit the dirt. Marion grabbed the crib with Holly inside and ducked around the back of the car. Agnes didn't stay down for long, and took aim with the shotgun.

'I've got your baby,' Marion blurted, unholstering the pistol Lyla had given her.

'What do I look like?' Agnes said, as she fired her shotgun over the car, endangering her own kid with a shower of lead pellets. 'You think I want that pooping scream-box hanging off my tit? What I want is a million for Robin Hood and two hundred grand for you and your wonky legs.'

Marion saw a shadowy figure stand up near to where Robin had been. She checked her surroundings as Agnes slowly walked around the car towards her. Marion saw that she only needed to back up a short distance to get cover behind the Marquee's decaying roadside billboard.

'Calm down, sweetie,' Marion told Holly as the tiny girl screamed her head off.

While Agnes moved away from the car, trying to get a clear shot, Marion held the crib in one hand, then stood up and shot wildly over the top of the car. First towards Agnes, then at the shadowy figure striding out of the bushes. She had no chance of hitting anything with wild one-handed shots, but it was enough to make them take cover.

Marion scrambled around the side of the sign. After a couple of seconds squatting behind it, she took a peek. Agnes and her pal didn't seem keen to go after Marion, so she decided the best thing to do was to get as far from the scene as possible, then figure out what to do next.

While Marion sprinted away with Holly, the man stepped out of cover. He wore a big smile as he carried Robin by the elastic waistband of his borrowed jogging pants, unconscious and with a tranquiliser dart sticking out of his butt.

'What's the old saying?' Guy Gisborne asked Agnes as he dropped Robin face down in the dirt. 'If you want a job done properly, do it yourself!'

As Agnes looked around to see where Marion had gone, Gisborne put two fingers in his mouth and whistled.

'Forget her,' Gisborne said. 'You're a rich lady now. The bounty on Marion Maid is chump change.'

'I know Marion,' Agnes said warily. 'Don't underestimate her.'

As Agnes glanced around, two tough guys came running in, drawn by their boss's whistle.

'Keep an eye out for Marion,' Gisborne warned them. 'We need to clear out of here and—'

'I'll head off,' Agnes said, pointing a thumb at the car. 'No point sticking around longer than I have to.'

'You can keep the car,' Gisborne told her as he stepped closer and offered his hand for Agnes to shake. 'Did you count the money in the trunk?'

Agnes laughed. 'Counting a million might take a while, but what I saw of it looked real enough.'

'Pleasure doing business,' Gisborne said, looking back to make sure Robin was still unconscious. He smiled and shook Agnes' hand, then after letting go he palmed a tiny tranquiliser gun from his trouser pocket and shot her twice. Once in the stomach, then in the neck as she hit the ground.

Gisborne looked at his two sidekicks. 'Mike, get the two suitcases of money from the trunk, then we'll take my car back into town. Zig, gag and cuff Agnes and drive her to Chief Constable Saetang's house in Queen's View.'

'Agnes tipped you off.' Mike laughed. 'That's harsh, boss.'

'Agnes is lucky I'm letting her live.' Gisborne wiped his muddy shoe across Agnes' chest. 'She did at least three robberies on my turf without cutting me in.'

Zig nodded. 'Am I taking Robin too?'

'No chance,' Gisborne said, scowling at Zig like that was the dumbest idea he'd ever heard. 'I'll be having some fun with that little brat before he dies.'

# 38. TONGUE-TEARERS

00:04

Marion ran away through the Marquee's parking lot, diving for cover when Mike and Zig ran in front of her.

When she reached the Marquee's overflow parking lot on the opposite side of the road, she recognised the customised Mercedes G-Wagon that Gisborne liked to call Black Bess II, parked among waist-high weeds.

'Oh no,' she gasped, as she realised who had just grabbed her best friend.

Marion put Holly's crib down and glanced to make sure nobody else was around. As she approached the boxy Mercedes, she pulled out the hunting knife she always carried in her front pocket and used it to stab both tyres on the driver's side.

She briefly considered an ambush when Gisborne and his men got back to the car. But while Robin might have been able to take out Gisborne, Agnes and two goons with his bow, Marion was sure she'd be outgunned with the pistol that Lyla had given her.

At least slashing the tyres would slow Gisborne's escape. Her next step was to let Rebel Control know what had happened. Even when the cops weren't switching the phone network on and off, it was tricky to get a mobile signal out here, so Marion went straight for the walkie-talkie clipped to her belt.

Except it wasn't clipped to her belt.

As Marion frantically patted her pockets, she remembered that they'd hidden her radio in Ken Stalin's suit trousers earlier in the day. And in all the chaos, she'd never asked for it back.

She felt sick with fear as she picked up Holly's crib and started to walk fast, not running because she didn't want to make a noise. She was pleased to get back to the two dirt bikes, but approached slowly, fearing that Gisborne had more people waiting for her.

It was a desperate situation, but Marion still took time to check and double-check the Velcro straps as she attached Holly's crib to the front of the bike. The five-week-old must have somehow sensed Marion's fear, because she seemed startled and oddly still.

'You're a good girl,' Marion said soothingly, straddling her bike. 'Nice and quiet.'

Marion had her thumb over the bike's starter button as she heard a car start, but she had a decision to make before setting off.

*Do I ride to the castle, or into town?*

*Normally I'd ride to the castle. But Azeem, Will and all the important rebels are at Locksley town hall. And Gisborne's based in Locksley, so if I head into town I'll likely be closer to wherever he's taking Robin.*

She hit 140 kph as she reached the elevated highway that ran into central Locksley. Her hair was going wild with no helmet and Holly was getting buffeted and started crying, but her priority was saving Robin. Every second mattered.

Even at high speed and with the constant fear of being wiped out by one of the highway's large potholes, Marion sensed that the city was calmer. Orange blazes had turned to smoky wisps, and the streets that ran below the highway were eerily empty.

Three kilometres from Locksley town hall, she decided to pull over and call Rebel Control. But the moment coincided with passing a cop car, parked on the hard shoulder.

As it turned out, the two officers had no interest in chasing a speeding dirt bike, but by the time Marion knew that, the overhead gantry signs were showing the turn-off for Central Square.

She felt scared and vulnerable as she slowed down: a forest kid who'd never navigated city streets alone. When she saw a sign *Town Hall Parking,* she turned left down a narrow alleyway, almost running over a frail homeless man pushing his belongings in a shopping trolley.

'Sorry!' she blurted, but kept riding.

At the bottom of the alleyway there were people in the street. Mostly student types, happily chanting 'Ardagh Hood'. Marion realised that Ardagh must have won, but she couldn't enjoy the victory while Robin was in danger.

The alleyway opened out into a wider street. A bunch of giant trash containers smouldered from an earlier fire. Marion felt sure she was behind Locksley town hall, but she couldn't see a way inside.

Just as Marion had convinced herself to turn the bike around, she spotted a ramp with a temporary sign at the top:

BALLOT BOX DELIVERIES: BAYS 4–6
CAR PARKING FOR ELECTION OFFICIALS ONLY

Marion flew down the ramp. At the bottom, she was surprised to see an enormous, armoured limousine parked. She feared the bike would get trashed or stolen, but she had no choice but to abandon it. She grabbed Holly's crib, then ran to a fire door that was jammed open and stepped into the back of the count room.

The rowdy crowd had dispersed after the result. The floor was covered in litter. Two caretakers were stacking the counting tables and the media was folding camera tripods and winding lengths of cable.

'Where is everyone?' Marion gasped as she spun around, hoping to spot a familiar face.

It seemed that Ardagh and his rebel security team were long gone. Marion recognised Oluchi Chanara, a journalist she'd met while liberating a group of hostage workers at a sneaker factory a year earlier, but what use would she be?

Marion was a wanted fugitive. Since an unaccompanied thirteen-year-old holding a baby in a crib at one in the morning was likely to draw attention, she leaned against a wall and hid her face as she pulled out her phone.

She was pleased to see a couple of signal bars, and decided to try the number for Rebel Control first. But as she scrolled through her contacts, a looming giant came at her from behind.

'Marion?' Little John said, making her jump. 'Why are you here? You'll get busted!'

'Gisborne's got Robin,' Marion blurted desperately. 'Is anyone still here? Azeem? Ísbjörg? Any of the Scarlocks?'

'Gisborne's people might cause trouble, so everyone split after the result. I'm just waiting for my driver to come out of the toilet.'

'Dammit,' Marion gasped, just as John's brain processed what she'd said.

'What do you mean, Gisborne's got Robin?'

'We were in the forest. Agnes McIntyre betrayed us. Robin got taken out with a tranquiliser dart. Probably by Gisborne himself.'

'You definitely saw Gisborne?'

'No, but I saw Black Bess II.'

'Who saw my dad's car?' Clare Gisborne asked as she walked up, shaking her wet hands and complaining, 'Not one paper towel in that bathroom.'

Marion held her hand over her gun, suddenly unsure whose side John was on.

'Your dad's got Robin,' John explained for Clare's benefit.

'That explains why he didn't show up here for the result,' Clare said, then she noticed Holly. 'Is that your baby?'

'I'm thirteen.' Marion tutted. 'Of course it's not.'

'We have to find Robin before your dad kills him,' John said, then looked at Clare. 'Where would your dad take him?'

'I slowed them down,' Marion interrupted. 'Slashed two of Black Bess's tyres.'

'Time *might* be on your side,' Clare said thoughtfully. 'My dad's a sadist who gets off on hurting people. He's been after Robin for months, so he won't just kill him. He'll whip and torment him for hours. Maybe even days.'

'Where would Gisborne take him?' John asked. 'Like, is there a torture chamber in your garden or something?'

'Dad's got places all over town, but my best guess would be Wally's Steakhouse,' Clare said. 'There's a private bar above the restaurant where my dad and his top cronies hang out playing darts. Often till three or four in the morning.

'There's a room at the back that my dad calls the Chokey. He collects weird antique stuff, like thumbscrews and medieval tongue-tearers. My mum says it's too creepy and won't let him have it in the house.'

'How far is Wally's from here?' Marion asked.

'Ten to twelve minutes by car,' Clare said.

'What car?' John pointed out, before looking at Marion. 'How did you get here?'

'Dirt bike. You're heavy, but I could squeeze you on for a short ride.'

Clare shook her head. 'The public part of the restaurant will be closed and the outside is all heavy metal doors and stuff. But if my dad's crew are still drinking upstairs, they'll let me in.'

'Tricky, tricky,' John mumbled to himself, as he gave a heavy sigh and glanced around. 'We need a car for three people, *and* I need to shed my close protection team.'

Marion glanced over at Oluchi in the crowd of reporters.

'There *might* be a way,' she said.

# 39. A GUY GISBORNE PRODUCTION

00:21

Robin felt a slap on the cheek, then an overpowering smell that made him think he was in the old chicken sheds at Sherwood Outlet Mall. But this ammonia stench wasn't from bird poop, it was a vial of smelling salts that Guy Gisborne had snapped under his nose.

'Wakey, wakey, brat!' Gisborne said.

Robin felt drowsy and nauseous. He realised he was lying on a cold tiled floor. His hands and ankles were tied with nylon fishing line that cut painfully into his skin, and the neck of his *Vote Ardagh* T-shirt had been ripped so that it hung off one shoulder.

As Robin blinked the blurriness out of his eyes, he saw Gisborne attaching a high-end mirrorless camera to a tripod.

'I thought I'd record our early-morning fun,' Gisborne purred. 'I just had a home cinema put in my basement.

I'll invite my boys round to play back your painful death on a five-metre screen in ultra high definition.'

Once the camera was on the tripod, Gisborne turned it on, then tutted. The battery was dead.

'That's Clare,' Gisborne snapped. 'Borrows my good camera for A level art and brings it back with a flat battery.'

As Gisborne rummaged in his camera bag for another battery, Robin tried to roll sideways because his wrists were trapped under his back and his fingers were numb. But the tiniest movement made the tightly wound fishing line dig excruciatingly into his wrists.

Robin moaned.

'You're not so tough,' Gisborne taunted. 'Did you hear your daddy won the election? But even if his win holds up in court, I still own the cops, judges, school board and planning department. The only thing Sheriff Hood will be able to do in my town is cop the blame when his do-gooder plans go wrong.'

'My dad's smarter than you think,' Robin said, trying to hide the strain in his voice.

'Finally,' Gisborne said as he found a working battery and clipped it to the camera.

Once he'd set the zoom and focus, Gisborne stood with his legs astride Robin. Then he put his hands under Robin's armpits, swept him easily off the ground and hung him from a ceiling hook by the elastic at the back of his tracksuit bottoms.

'Nice wedgie.' Gisborne laughed as the oversized tracksuit bottoms stretched, leaving Robin dangling horizontally over the tiled floor.

Gisborne picked up a small *sjambok* whip and brought it down against Robin's back with enough force to shred his T-shirt.

'A little beauty, this one,' Gisborne said, as Robin cried in pain. 'Made from rhino skin over a hundred years ago for French colonial police, but still wonderfully effective.'

Robin didn't want to show weakness but a tear streaked down his cheek, much to Gisborne's amusement.

'Crying after one lick!' Gisborne smiled. 'That was the first of hundreds. I've got an entire whip collection to try on you. By tomorrow you'll be begging me to let you die.'

As Robin sobbed, Gisborne gave an excited jump, like a kid waiting for presents on Christmas Eve.

'Breaking you will be fun,' Gisborne said. He strode across the room and picked up Robin's bow. 'And since my face and this grotty room are the last things you'll ever see, you'll not be needing this again.'

Gisborne held Robin's bow at one end, then swung it with all his might against the top of a battered metal workbench. The bow's taut cable made a noisy ping, and the weapon's carbon fibre body disintegrated into hundreds of pieces.

Gisborne clearly hadn't realised that carbon fibre shattered on heavy impact. Robin turned his head and closed his eyes as shards of razor-sharp carbon flew in all directions. Since Gisborne was holding the bow, his face and torso caught most of the shards and he stumbled back, holding his face.

The biggest chunk of Robin's bow spun off sideways, crashing into the tripod. This knocked Gisborne's expensive camera against a side wall with enough force to snap off the lens at the weak spot where it joined the camera body.

'Aaargh!' Gisborne yelled, as he dived in to save the camera.

Robin hurt in ten places, but he still teased Gisborne. 'You can put that in out-takes at the end of your movie.'

Gisborne turned to face Robin, his eyes furious and with carbon fibre shrapnel in his beard.

'I'll wipe off your smile, Hood,' Gisborne growled, then grabbed the tripod with the broken camera on the end and swung it like a golf club, smashing Robin in the ribs.

Robin couldn't breathe as the powerful blow lifted his body clean off the hook. With his wrists tied behind his back, he crashed to the hard floor, unable to protect his face. Pain shot through his body. Although even tiny movements were excruciating, instinct made him roll onto his side and pull his knees up to his chest.

As Gisborne roared with fury and staggered around looking through the debris for his *sjambok*, Robin felt a shard of carbon fibre digging into the back of his hand.

If he could turn his hand over, he might be able to pick it up. And if it was sharp, maybe it would cut the fine nylon fishing line that Gisborne had wound around his wrists . . .

# 40. VAN ON THE RUN

00:38

'It'll be a miracle if I don't get fired for this,' twenty-something reporter Oluchi said as she drove the orange Channel 9 news van around the side of Locksley town hall with Marion in the outside front passenger seat, Holly's crib in the middle and Clare Gisborne in the back amidst racks of satellite transmission equipment, aluminium flight cases and Marion's mud-splattered dirt bike.

'You know like in the movies?' Marion said, trying to make a joke to break the tension. 'When the TV van goes under a low bridge and it tears the giant satellite dish off the roof?'

'Channel 9 gives me a pension plan and six weeks' paid leave,' Oluchi said. 'But maybe I'll win a journalism award if we rescue Robin Hood . . .'

Then Oluchi hit the brakes hard enough for something heavy to fall off a rack in the rear compartment. As she stopped at the kerb, she saw Little John's chunky shoulders squeezing through a window at the back of a gents toilet.

Clare opened the van's sliding side door. John dropped from the window and jumped in, then Oluchi shot off, making the van's tyres squeal.

'Who knows where Wally's is?' Oluchi asked.

'Left onto the 107, then turn off at junction six,' Clare shouted from the back.

But left took them towards a little street market, where a hefty barricade had been built by shopkeepers and stallholders to stop looting. Oluchi had to reverse up the narrow lane, then she drove straight while Clare studied the map on her phone.

'Next left if it's clear,' Clare said.

Marion saw cops at the side of the road, brandishing their stun batons over a bunch of drunk-looking students in *Vote Ardagh* T-shirts.

After ten minutes they had reached Wally's, where they were pleased to see lights on upstairs and a parking lot with a row of the kind of fancy cars you can afford if you're high up in Gisborne's organisation.

The orange van with the Channel 9 news logo and a satellite dish on the roof wasn't exactly discreet, so Oluchi parked it outside a betting shop a few doors down.

'I'll go inside with John,' Clare said.

'Leave your phone on speaker,' Oluchi said.

'Eh?' John said.

'Call me,' Oluchi explained. 'Then leave your phone on speaker and we should be able to hear what's going on.'

'Clever,' Marion said as she pulled her holstered pistol over her head. 'One of you had better take this as well.'

'I've only held a gun, like, twice,' John said.

'My dad used to take me to the shooting range,' Clare said. She took the gun, expertly removed the clip, checked the chamber, then shoved the weapon in her trouser pocket. 'My dad's crew won't dare search me.'

'Be safe,' Oluchi warned as they set off.

As they got close to Wally's sliding glass doors, John called Oluchi, put his phone on speaker and slid it into his jacket pocket.

The restaurant's metal grilles were down, but there were two women inside polishing the leather booths and a guy at the bar unloading racks of steaming glassware from a commercial dishwasher.

'Closed for tonight,' one of the women yelled, wagging a finger as Clare neared the door.

'I'm Clare, Clare Gisborne,' she said, as John noticed a flash of orange indicator lights behind him. He looked around and saw a guy in a leather jacket unlocking a little BMW coupe.

'Miss Gisborne,' the guy emptying the dishwasher said, sprinting to unlock the door. 'Sorry, sorry! What's the matter? Why are you kids out so late?'

As dishwasher guy unlocked the restaurant, John half-watched the man in the leather jacket struggling to load two large roll bags into the BMW. Given the reputation of Gisborne's gang, he wondered if it was a body sawn in half.

'I dropped by to see my dad before I went back to school,' Clare explained.

Dishwasher guy shook his head. 'I've not seen Mr Gisborne today. I'm not sure where he is.'

'Really?' Clare said, acting confused. 'Could my dad have come in the back way or something? I was told he'd be here.'

The man pointed past the bar to an open kitchen. 'Front or back, there's only one set of stairs to the top room. I would have seen him.'

'Right,' Clare said uncertainly. 'Crossed wires, I guess. Are the guys still drinking upstairs? I can't get my dad's mobile, but one of them might know where we can find him.'

'Go ahead and ask,' the guy said.

Clare led John up narrow stairs with knackered green carpet. There was a push button lock on the door at the top, but Clare knew the code. She stepped into a cosy bar with a pool table and two dartboards. Four of Gisborne's top guys stood around a well-stocked bar where the customers served themselves.

There was cigar smoke in the air and a joke going down, but the unnerving presence of the boss's daughter and her boyfriend killed the banter.

'I thought I was meeting my dad here,' Clare said awkwardly, as she tried to remember the names of her dad's cronies. 'With everything going nuts, we must have got our wires crossed. And I can't get through to his phone.'

'Starkey knows where the boss is,' a guy Clare was pretty sure was called Roger said. 'He came in and picked up some stuff that the boss wanted from the Chokey.'

'If Starkey can squeeze it in that stupid little car of his,' another guy said, earning laughs from his mates.

'Chokey?' John said. 'Like in the book *Matilda*? The place where the headmistress sends kids to be punished?'

The four guys shrugged and looked at each other, like they'd never read a book in their lives.

'The boss collects some wild stuff,' a guy holding a huge glass of brandy said. 'It's not locked. Stick your head in and have a butcher's.'

The guy pointed John to a door, and he went to look.

The Chokey was a windowless storage area about eight metres by five. The walls were lined with illuminated glass cabinets. Inside were all sorts of horrible pointy things for tearing, gouging and chopping bits off human bodies, while Gisborne's whip collection ran the entire length of the back wall.

'Is Starkey around?' Clare said to the guys at the bar. 'He must know where my dad is.'

As John stepped further into the Chokey, he realised that this wasn't Gisborne's torture chamber, but the place where Gisborne used his creepy collection to impress friends, or intimate enemies. He also noticed that a lot of the whips were missing from their hooks, and one was on the floor, as if someone had grabbed them in a hurry.

'You just missed Starkey,' the brandy-drinker said.

'Cherry-red BMW coupe,' John said, hoping that Marion and Oluchi could hear on speakerphone as he stepped back into the bar area. 'I think I saw him putting stuff in the car as we arrived.'

Clare gave a fake yawn and looked at John. 'I'm beat, and it sounds like my dad's busy. I'm gonna head home and sleep.'

'We'll let your dad know you were looking for him if he calls,' Roger said. 'Have you got a ride?'

'My driver's waiting,' John said, as Clare headed for the exit.

'Do you think those guys know my dad's got Robin?' Clare whispered as the pair rushed down the stairs.

'Maybe,' John said.

They hurried through the restaurant. John pulled out his phone the instant they were in the night air.

'How much did you hear?' John asked Oluchi, as the young reporter reversed the satellite truck to the edge of Wally's car park.

'Enough to know that I need to follow a red BMW,' Oluchi answered. John and Clare sprinted towards the van.

'Lucky for us, Starkey took ages getting all the stuff in his car and setting his satnav,' Marion added. 'He turned towards the centre of town. If he sticks to the main road and Oluchi puts her foot down, we should be able to catch him up.'

# 41. CHERRY-RED COUPE

00:57

Oluchi took a risk, running a red light and catching the BMW coupe at the next junction. They were cruising in the dark, passing rows of identical abandoned apartment blocks that had once housed workers at Locksley's auto plants.

'Starkey can't be going far if he's not taking the highway,' Clare noted.

The trouble was, at one in the morning there was no traffic, and Starkey would surely realise he was being followed by a bright orange van with a dish on the roof. Oluchi stayed back as far as she dared, but they lost the BMW when it came off the main road and took a couple of quick turns.

'Now what?' Oluchi grumbled, thumping her steering wheel as she stopped at a T-junction. 'Left or right? It's a fifty-fifty chance.'

'And Robin dies if we get it wrong,' John said.

'Dirt bike,' Marion blurted, looking at John and Clare in the back. 'We'll split up.'

Clare opened the van's back door. John's strength came in handy as he easily lifted Marion's bike out.

'Keep an eye on Holly,' Marion yelled, straddling the bike as van doors slammed.

Oluchi went left, so Marion took a right, and found herself passing a strip of auto workshops and dodgy second-hand car dealerships. After those, the road narrowed to a cobbled lane, with moonlight catching the Macondo River at the far end.

She'd entered the oldest part of Locksley's docks. The industrial buildings had been laid out in narrow alleyways in the days when cargo arrived on sail barges. Most were in a shocking state of repair and some were burnt out, leaving only a brick shell.

At this time in the morning, the area was a creepy maze. There were dozens of alleyways between buildings, though luckily for Marion most were too narrow for Starkey's BMW.

Riding over cobbles was jarring, and Marion felt sure she'd wasted her time when she hit a waterfront path, separated by a line of bollards too tight for a car to pass through. But as she turned the bike around, headlights lit up a passageway between two buildings as a car sped down the alleyway at its far end.

The passage gave less than ten centimetres' clearance for Marion's handlebars, so she had to take it slow. By the time she reached the end, she could only see the car's vanishing rear lights.

Marion hadn't seen enough to identify the red coupe, but the engine's roar suggested a sporty car. And since there was no reason to drive down here unless you were dropping something off, Marion decided it was better to try and work out where the car had been, rather than chase it.

She twisted her handlebars slowly, turning the dirt bike's headlamp into a searchlight and scanning the narrow alleyway, with hulking brick buildings on either side.

Marion slowly rode back where the car had come from. At the end of this alleyway, she found herself on a broad stretch of riverfront. There were a couple of burnt-out cars, a dock where two barges had rusted until they sank, and colonies of birds perched on abandoned dock cranes.

As she aimed her headlight along the dockside, it lit up a tatty beige estate car. It looked like the one Agnes had been sitting on before Robin was captured – and it made sense that Gisborne would have used it, because she'd slashed the tyres of his Mercedes.

'Robin's close,' Marion told herself.

She assumed Gisborne wouldn't have wanted to carry Robin any further than he had to, which meant they'd likely be in one of two identical warehouse buildings closest to the parked car. These waterfront buildings were shabby, but in better shape than the ones in the alleyways behind.

Both were four storeys tall, with facades stretching fifty metres along the river. Part of their original frontage had been knocked out and replaced with a glass lobby.

Marion switched the bike's headlight off, then rolled it back into the alleyway. As she pulled out her phone, she felt anxious.

*32% battery and five signal bars. Yay!*

But as she scrolled through her contacts, Marion had the horrible realisation that she'd split from the others in a hurry, and she didn't have a number for John, Clare or Oluchi.

# 42. CORPORATE COMMUNICATION POLICY

01:19

'No, no! *Please* listen,' Marion begged into her phone. 'I'm calling your newsroom because I need to urgently contact Oluchi Chanara about a story she's working on.'

'I understood the first time,' the man on the other end of the line said robotically. 'But the Channel 9 news desk is not authorised to hand out the mobile numbers of reporters to every random person who calls at 1am. If you give me a message and your contact details, I will forward these to Miss Chanara by email.'

'You're useless!' Marion growled. She hung up and felt like throwing her phone at the ground.

*Who do I know who'd have a number for Clare or John? Who, who, who . . .*

Then Marion was struck by a brainwave. Robin and John's Auntie Pauline would have John's number. Marion didn't have Pauline's number, but she *did* have her own Aunt Lucy's number. And Lucy had known Pauline for years.

'Sure, I have Pauline's number,' Lucy said. 'But why do you need it at one in the morning? Where are you?'

'No time to explain, Auntie,' Marion said. 'Text me that number, now!'

Marion's frustration hit a new peak when her call to Pauline cut to voicemail, but Pauline called straight back with John's number.

'John!' Marion gasped with relief when he answered. 'I think I know where they are. Well, not exactly, but I've narrowed it down to a couple of buildings.'

'Oluchi reckons we're less than ten minutes away,' John said after Marion had explained everything. 'And call your rebel friends too. We'll probably need back-up.'

Marion was about to call Rebel Control when she noticed a row of lights flick on, inside the second floor of the warehouse on the left. They stayed on for around twenty seconds, then it went dark before they came back on for another twenty, like they were on a timed switch.

The angle from the waterfront was too steep for Marion to see anyone moving inside, but another light came on at the far end of the building. It was definitely a kitchen because the back of a fridge partly blocked one window. After about the time it takes to make a cup of tea, the kitchen light went out and the timed switch in the hallway came back on.

At the opposite end of the second floor, Marion's eye was drawn to a corner room. It had black shutters at all the windows, apart from one at the side, which had been replaced by an air conditioning unit. Unlike all the other rusty air-cons hanging off the side of the warehouse, this one was spinning.

Marion was about to try calling Rebel Control again when the satellite van came barrelling down the alleyway.

'I checked the property register on the way here,' Clare said, getting out of the van as Marion looked in the front to check on Holly. 'One of my dad's companies owns the building on the left.'

'I think Gisborne's there,' Marion said, as she pointed up. 'See the weird room at the end, second floor, with shutters over the windows?'

'Air conditioning's running,' Oluchi noted smartly.

Clare looked at Marion. 'Any sign of someone else up there with my dad?'

Marion shrugged. 'We can't be sure.'

As Marion spoke, they caught the sound of another car coming towards them. She hurriedly wheeled her bike out of sight into an alcove. Clare squatted down next to her, while Oluchi and John got back in the satellite van.

'Starkey's back,' Clare said, as his cherry-red BMW slowed to a crawl to get through the narrow gap between the orange van and the brick buildings.

As Starkey parked beside the beige estate car, Clare and Marion peeked out along the waterfront. Starkey was fuming as he reached into his boot for a camera bag and tripod. He was mumbling under his breath, but the sound carried far enough for Clare and Marion to catch most of it.

'Fifty years old and still His Majesty's errand boy,' Starkey moaned. 'And Gisborne will still expect me to be out making collections first thing . . .'

Clare smirked while Starkey walked to the warehouse's main lobby and jabbed at a button on the entry panel.

'If my dad heard him talk like that, he'd chop him up and feed him to his pigs,' Clare whispered to Marion.

The door's entry buzzer sounded. As Starkey dashed inside with the replacement camera and tripod, Clare and Marion walked back to the satellite van.

'I don't think Starkey clocked us,' Oluchi said.

'This van's bright orange,' John said warily. 'He must have noticed us following him earlier.'

'Starkey's in a mood, probably tired too,' Marion noted.

Oluchi and John's phones gave a dramatic little trumpet notification at the same instant. Marion peered around John's arm as he tapped on a notification and read aloud.

'Channel 9 newsflash. Marjorie Kovacevic is new president, as final result shows bigger than expected 56 to 44 victory. Click to watch live video as our new leader is driven to the Presidential Palace to be sworn in.'

'Like this country wasn't messed up enough already,' Marion complained, then looked awkwardly at John. 'No offence.'

John shrugged. 'When I turn eighteen, I won't be voting for my mum.'

'Forget the election and stay on task,' Oluchi said firmly. 'Robin's up there, probably being whipped and tortured as we speak. Gisborne might kill him if he hears us coming. How can we get him out safely?'

# 43. HAPPY EVER AFTER

01:35

Starkey was on his phone as he came out of the warehouse. 'On my way home now, babe . . . Who says I'm partying at Wally's? I told you, Gisborne's had me running errands. If he calls again, I'm not answering. Tell him my battery died, or something . . . Hold on!'

Starkey stopped talking because he'd seen Clare Gisborne leaning against his car. 'Why are you—'

Before Starkey got his question out, a figure jumped from behind him and wrapped a huge arm around his neck. Clare had done martial arts all her life, and gave Starkey a savage knee in the stomach.

'Where are your weapons?' Clare demanded as Starkey coughed and retched.

As John held Starkey upright, Clare slugged him in the gut. 'Answer me, now.'

'Jack— jacket,' Starkey rasped, a big string of snot dropping from his nose.

Marion and Oluchi strode up as Clare unzipped Starkey's leather jacket and took out a holstered gun.

'Take this,' Clare said, passing Starkey's gun to Marion. Then she patted him down and found a wallet in the back of his jeans and a folding knife in the front.

'What is this?' Starkey asked breathlessly.

Clare unfolded Starkey's knife and held it in front of his face. 'I ask questions, you answer,' she said firmly. 'Is my dad upstairs?'

'Sure.'

'With Robin Hood?'

'Sure.'

'Anyone else? Bodyguard, security officer, whatever?'

'Nobody that I saw. But why are you on their side?'

Clare gave Starkey another punch in the gut. 'I kinda like hurting people,' she growled nastily. 'Must have got that from my dad. Just try and remember: I ask questions, you answer them. Is Robin in the room at the end of the second floor?'

'I didn't see. The boss met me at the top of the stairs.'

'But you just said Robin's there.'

'I could hear him.'

'What was he saying?'

'Nothing. He was crying in pain because your dad's been working him over.'

'Here's what you're going to do, Starkey,' Clare said. 'Take a few breaths and get your head together. Then you're going to buzz my dad. Tell him you dropped your car keys on the way downstairs. You need to get back in to look for them.'

'Please, Clare. Your dad will kill me.'

Clare flashed the knife. 'I'll kill you if you don't.'

'Your dad will come after you as well,' Starkey spat. 'But if you let me go now, we can pretend none of this ever happened.'

'Do you want more?' Clare said, as she bunched her fist. 'I'm not running a debating club.'

Marion pocketed Starkey's phone and wallet and John shoved him towards the entry panel. Starkey's hand trembled as he pushed the button.

'Mr Stark?' Gisborne said cheerfully after a few seconds.

Starkey sounded shaky, but Gisborne bought his story about dropping his car keys and buzzed him in.

John let Starkey go as they stepped into the musty lobby. There was a sign with an alphabetical list of companies that used the building, but the dirty floor and lift with *out of order* sign suggested the place got few visitors.

'Marion,' Clare said quietly. 'You stay down here. Point the gun at Starkey and shoot him if he moves or makes a noise. Oluchi, wait outside and let us know if anyone else shows up.'

Clare pulled out the gun that Marion had given her at Wally's, then began creeping up the staircase that wrapped around the lift shaft, with John behind.

'You're awesome,' John whispered. 'Putting my brother before your dad.'

'I don't want to shoot my dad,' Clare said. 'I'm hoping he doesn't want to shoot me and we can make him let Robin go.'

John smiled, unconvinced. 'And we'll all live happily ever after.'

When they reached the second floor, Clare kept low as she leaned out of the stairwell.

To her left the corridor went twenty metres, with rooms off to the side and the little kitchen at the far end. At the opposite end there was the corner room. Its metal door was slightly ajar, with light leaking around the edges. They could hear crying and sobs that gave John chills.

'Now what?' he whispered.

Before Clare could answer, the light coming out of the door increased until Gisborne stood silhouetted in the doorway.

'Just going for a tinkle, kid,' Gisborne told Robin cheerily. 'You know, I'm enjoying this so much I might not kill you at all. I can keep you in my wine cellar and get you out for a good whipping on special occasions.'

Gisborne laughed at his own joke as he punched the timed light switch and headed down the hallway.

'Find your keys, Starkey?' Gisborne shouted, practically skipping with joy. John and Clare backed down the stairs and out of sight.

Clare tensed up, thinking she might have to pull a gun on her dad. But when Gisborne reached the stairs, he crossed to the other side of the lift shaft and took the flight going up. Clare and John realised they now had an opportunity to grab Robin while Gisborne peed. With luck, they might even clear out before he got back.

The instant her dad was out of sight, Clare shot out of the staircase and dashed towards the room at the far end, John right behind.

'You get Robin, I'll cover with the gun,' Clare said. 'And hurry!'

John wasn't prepared for what he saw as he stepped into the room. He choked up when he saw Robin. He was barely conscious, facing the wall, dangling by his wrists, his back and legs bloody from being whipped.

'No more, please,' Robin sobbed. John reached up and started undoing the leather wrist straps.

'It's me, John,' he said, trying to soothe his little brother, but at the same time so furious that he wanted to explode.

'Come on!' Clare pleaded from outside.

As John freed the first wrist strap, Robin's entire body weight shifted onto his other wrist. John tried to take Robin's weight, but his torso was bloody and slippery, and John lost his grip.

Robin cried out in pain.

'Sorry, mate,' John said, choking back tears.

'Tell him to be quiet,' Clare said, as John dragged a chair across the room.

'Stand on the chair,' John told Robin, then got to work on the second wrist strap.

'John, is that really you?' Robin asked, close to losing consciousness.

'I've got you,' John said as he unfastened the buckle of the second wrist strap and let Robin's body droop over his shoulder. 'Clare, let's go!'

Every movement made Robin's wounds hurt and he flopped like a doll as John carried him into the hallway.

'The state of him!' Clare gasped when she saw Robin.

'He can barely talk,' John said. 'We need to get him to a clinic.'

Clare led them back towards the stairs, but they were still a few metres shy when the lights in the hallway came on.

'Traitor!' Gisborne roared at Clare, aiming his gun straight at her head.

# 44. Y'ALL AIN'T GOT GUTS

01:48

'My own flesh and blood,' Gisborne sneered, pointing his gun as Clare pointed hers back at him. 'What happened to you?'

'Don't get any closer,' Clare said anxiously. The timed hallway light clicked off, throwing them back into darkness.

'Where's my girl?' Gisborne demanded. 'The one who smashed every boy at ju-jitsu? The one who wanted to grow up and be just like Daddy?'

'She grew up,' Clare snarled back. 'She started thinking for herself. She decided it's not right to have a dad who slaps his wife and buys hamsters for his eight-year-old son to shoot with an air pistol.'

'I feel pain every day where Robin shot me,' Gisborne said, as he took another step. 'And you don't have the guts to pull that trigger on your old man.'

'Mum already wants a divorce,' Clare spat back. 'If you kill me, she'll do it. Then all you'll have left are your pathetic monkey slaves, standing around in Wally's, laughing at your rubbish jokes.'

Gisborne eyed John, who still carried Robin over his shoulder.

'I'll take out Robin and lover boy with one shot. I'll wound you, then lock you in your room until you learn some respect.'

Clare snorted. 'President Marjorie will *crush* you if you shoot her son.'

'Maybe she'll never find out it was me,' Gisborne said, taking another step towards Clare, so that their guns almost touched.

'Just let us walk out with Robin,' John said. 'Call it even. Nobody needs to get shot.'

'And now the great lump speaks,' Gisborne said, smirking. 'You're a useless zit, Hood. Like your brother and your father.'

'The useless zit who just beat you in an election,' John bit back.

Gisborne heard footsteps on the staircase. John guessed it was Marion.

'Stay back!' Gisborne warned.

Gisborne glanced nervously back towards the staircase. Robin coughed. The movement made him moan in pain, and his bloody body slid from John's grasp.

'Whoa,' John said, instinctively stepping sideways so he didn't drop Robin.

But the hallway was dark. Gisborne was on edge because someone was coming at him from behind, and now he assumed that John was coming for him.

As Gisborne took aim towards John and Robin, Clare sensed what was about to happen and lunged forward, hitting her dad's arm. This forced Gisborne's shot to go wide, and the bullet shattered one of the hallway windows.

Clare's momentum made her stumble into the hallway wall. Gisborne kept upright and corrected his aim for another shot at John.

'Dad, no!' Clare yelled.

As John threw Robin away from the line of fire, Gisborne took aim from point-blank range. But two perfectly targeted shots came from back near the stairs. Gisborne's heart exploded before he could pull the trigger. His head exploded half a second later.

'Jesus!' Clare screamed as she looked towards the stairs.

She expected Marion, but Officer Scott and another close protection officer named Phuong were coming down from the floor above. They both held assault rifles. As John rolled onto his back, the red dot from Phuong's laser sight jiggled across his chest.

'Weapons down!' Scott screamed, while Phuong pushed on the timer switch that lit up the hallway. 'Do it, NOW!'

Clare dropped her pistol as Phuong closed her down.

'We have John,' Scott yelled into his police radio. Then he saw the blood smeared over John's shirt. 'Are you injured?'

'It's Robin's blood,' John explained. 'Maybe a spattering of Gisborne's too.'

As Phuong ordered Clare to sit against the wall with her hands on her head, Scott saw Robin, slumped on the floor where John had thrown him, his clothes shredded and bloody whip marks all over his body.

'He's in a proper state,' Scott said, then spoke to the third member of his team by radio. 'Catherine, get up here with the medical kit from the limo. I have Robin Hood, but he's a bloody mess. Call an ambulance too. Make sure they know it's a top-priority request for the president's close protection team.'

As Oluchi snuck around the top of the stairs filming on her phone, Phuong unravelled a foil blanket and threw it over what was left of Guy Gisborne.

'You – scram!' Scott yelled to Oluchi furiously.

'I am an accredited journalist filming a crime scene, as is my right under Article 7 of the Constitution,' Oluchi announced.

'OK,' Scott said grudgingly. 'But you stay back by the stairs. One step nearer and I'll arrest you for interfering with a crime scene.'

As Officer Catherine came off the stairs and ran past Oluchi with the medical bag, Scott squatted down beside John.

'How did you find me?' John asked.

'We never lost sight of you,' said Scott proudly. 'I've had two years' close protection training and seven years on the job. It'll take more than squeezing your fat arse out of a back window if you want to lose me.'

John glanced at the crackling foil blanket over Gisborne. 'With hindsight, I'm glad you kept up with me.'

'When you snuck away, I thought you were planning to make out with your girlfriend, not charge all over town and get in a shootout.'

Robin moaned as Catherine knelt beside him. 'Hey there, pal. Can you hear me?'

'Sure,' Robin croaked weakly.

'You've got five or six wounds that will probably need stitches. But for now, I'm going to cut away what's left of your T-shirt and wind a compression bandage around your chest. It will be uncomfortable, so I'll give you an injection to numb the pain first.'

As Catherine ripped off the Velcro cover of her medical bag, Scott looked her way while pointing his thumb back at Oluchi. 'We've got Channel 9 watching, so you'd better do this by the book.'

'He's just a kid.' Catherine sighed, and pulled a roll of elastic bandage out of the bag. 'Look at the state of him.'

Officer Phuong sounded mad. 'That kid you're so fond of is wanted for shooting cops and murdering a prison officer,' she said, walking towards Robin. 'I'll read the monster his rights if you don't want to.'

Catherine rolled her eyes as she rummaged through the medical bag. 'Knock yourself out.'

'Robin Hood, you are under arrest,' Phuong began. 'As you are under sixteen years old, we cannot question you or record anything you say until a parent, guardian or court-appointed representative is present. Do you understand?'

John charged forward as Robin murmured something indecipherable. 'You're arresting him?'

Scott stepped into John's path and tried to calm him down. 'We're police officers, and your brother is a wanted criminal. But don't worry, I won't let the pitiful excuse for a police force they have here in Locksley get near him.'

John felt like punching something as he backed up to the wall, then he caught sight of his girlfriend. Phuong had let Clare stand up after being searched, and she was now tearful and shocked. Oluchi filmed discreetly on her phone as John pulled her into a tight hug.

'This might be good for Robin,' Clare suggested. 'It was only a matter of time before he got himself killed. And I heard that the longest sentence they can give a kid is ten years.'

'Sorry about your dad,' John said tearfully.

'I still loved him,' Clare admitted. 'At least, in a way.'

'It's confusing,' John said. 'Like with my mum . . .'

As Robin got his painkilling injection, Scott's phone rang.

'Scottie here!' he answered casually. But his tone stiffened when he realised who was on the other end. 'Good morning, Madam President. How may I be of assistance?'

# 45. PEACH AND LOVE

02:26

Clare and John stood together in the second-floor hallway, holding hands, as an ambulance pulled up on the waterfront. Scott had just ended his call with the newly elected president.

'What did my mum say?' John asked.

Scott sounded flustered. 'The president is delighted. She thinks that having her close protection team arrest Robin Hood less than an hour after she is sworn in makes her look good. Channel 9 is already broadcasting the story. The rest of the media won't be far behind, so we can expect a circus out front in minutes.'

'But I led you to Robin,' John said. 'You had no idea I was looking for Robin.'

'Politics is all spin,' Scott said. 'When people get out of bed in the morning, the headline will be *Marjorie elected,*

*Robin arrested.* By the time all the details get out, nobody will care.'

A male and female paramedic ran up the stairs and took over Catherine's job looking after Robin. The protection officer looked shaken as she peeled off disposable gloves smeared with Robin's blood.

'How's my brother doing?' John asked.

'The deeper whip marks on his back will need stitches, and he might have some broken ribs,' Catherine said. 'But he's young and fit. He should heal fast.'

'Tell those paramedics to move Robin out of here ASAP,' Scott said. 'This town is a powder keg, and arresting Robin could easily spark trouble.'

'There's only three of us,' Phuong said. 'We should call local cops for assistance.'

'I don't trust Locksley police,' Scott said, almost spitting with contempt. 'And don't forget, half of 'em are on the payroll of the man *you* just shot.'

The paramedics had given Robin an oxygen mask to make breathing easier, and he moaned into it gently as they rolled him onto a stretcher.

'You're heavy for a little guy!' the female paramedic said.

John went after the paramedics as they stretchered Robin towards the stairs.

'Stay!' Scott said, pulling John back. 'You and Clare are getting straight in the limo. We'll drop Clare home. The president wants you in Capital City, stepping onto that balcony at sunrise.'

'No way,' John said. 'I'm going with Robin in the ambulance.'

'Robin is under arrest,' Scott said firmly. 'The police and paramedics will take him.'

John panicked, as he realised it might be months before he was allowed to see Robin in prison.

'Can I at least walk down with him and say goodbye?'

'Go for it,' Scott said, then looked back at his two colleagues. 'I'll go in the ambulance with Robin. Catherine, you drive Clare and John in the limousine. Phuong, stay here. Cordon off the stairs and keep the press and local cops out of the building. I've requested forensics and support officers from the National Police, but they're an hour away.'

John and Scott quickly caught up with the paramedics carrying the stretcher downstairs. Robin seemed more chilled, but his eyes were glassy. When he saw John, he lifted up his oxygen mask.

'Little John!' Robin said. 'I love you, man.'

'Is he OK?' John asked.

'Three shots of pain meds,' the paramedic holding the back of the stretcher explained. 'They can make you a little loopy.'

'John, I've got something to tell you,' Robin said, as the stretcher went around the first-floor landing.

'Robin, keep that oxygen mask on,' the paramedic at the front urged. 'Deep breaths will help you relax and ease the pain.'

'Gisborne smashed my bow,' Robin said, his words slurring. 'I'm never getting another one. I'm never shooting anyone again.'

'Peace and love,' John said, managing a smile. 'Maybe that vibe will suit you.'

'Peach and love,' Robin sang. 'Peach aaaaaaand love.'

# 46. CAN'T FEEL A THING

02:38

'Mask on, Robin,' the male paramedic repeated, as the stretcher reached the ground-floor lobby.

Oluchi and a couple of freshly arrived media folk backed up to the wall as the stretcher came through. Outside, three more stood between the lobby's glass door and the ambulance parked on the waterfront, while a camera operator broke into a sprint when he realised he was about to miss Robin's exit.

'Back it up, idiots!' Scott shouted, as two video lights blinded him. 'Let the ambulance crew do their job.'

'Little John,' a random journalist shouted. 'Is it true you sold out your brother?'

'Print that and I'll knock your teeth down your throat,' John roared.

John rarely lost his temper, but he was exhausted and the state he'd found Robin in had made something snap.

Three steps later, a TV camera got in John's face and he whacked it so hard that the camera person stumbled back and fell to the cobbles.

'Cool it,' Scott told John. 'Lashing out won't help.'

Though to be fair, nobody came within two metres of John once they'd seen how strong he was.

'Are you police?' a woman shouted to Scott. 'Can you confirm the Channel 9 report that Guy Gisborne is dead?'

'No comment!' Scott said, as a paramedic opened the back of the ambulance. 'If you want information, call the National Police press office.'

Officer Catherine and Clare had followed John down the stairs.

'Let's get you two in the limo and out of this scrum,' Catherine urged.

The media got in the paramedics' way as they pulled a wheeled trolley from the back of the ambulance. They raised Robin's stretcher onto it, then rolled him inside. At the front of the ambulance, the driver blasted her siren to make a News 24 satellite truck back out of the way.

'I can't stay with you, mate,' John shouted to Robin. 'Get better, I'll see you soon.'

'Cheerio!' Robin yelled.

John tried leaning into the ambulance to squeeze Robin's hand, but he couldn't reach so he squeezed his filthy big toe instead.

'Right,' Catherine said, rubbing John's back as a tear streaked down his cheek. 'Let's get to the car.'

'I love your stupid hairy face, John Bon,' Robin shouted.

'Drive!' the female paramedic yelled, getting a camera flash in the face as she hopped in the ambulance and pulled the back door closed.

As the ambulance weaved slowly along the waterfront between TV vans and journalists' cars, Scott squashed himself into a flip-down passenger seat by the rear doors. The female paramedic pulled safety straps over Robin, while the man opened an overhead cabinet and pulled out a syringe.

'Another shot, I'm afraid,' the paramedic told Robin as he peeled off the syringe's sterile packaging. 'This one's an antibiotic to stop you getting a nasty infection.'

'I'm in an amber-lance!' Robin sang, his head flopping to one side. 'Nee-naw, nee-naw, nee-naw.'

The ambulance sped up and the siren came on for real as it left the old docks and headed for the highway.

'Three news drones and a helicopter following us,' the driver announced from up front. 'I hope we're getting good ratings.'

'Live, tonight, sold out!' Robin said, then snickered as the paramedic unwrapped another syringe. 'Peach and love. Where's my John gone?'

'Your brother will see you soon,' the paramedic said as he passed the syringe over Robin to the paramedic standing by the back doors near Scott.

'Officer, I need to put this needle into Robin's ankle,' the female paramedic explained. 'Since we're a bit squeezed in, would you mind shuffling forward in your seat and putting gentle pressure on Robin's right ankle? It's just to stop him jerking when it goes in.'

'Happy to help,' Scott said, leaning forward and pushing down on Robin's leg. 'Like this?'

'I need cheese!' Robin said. 'I'm a hungry hungry hippo.'

'Nice and still, Robin,' the male paramedic said.

'That's perfect, Officer, thank you,' the female paramedic said. But instead of putting the needle in Robin's leg, she plunged it in the back of Scott's neck.

'No . . .' Scott roared, trying to reach for his gun. But the male paramedic stepped in and the pair of them pinned Scott's head to the edge of Robin's stretcher.

After a brief struggle, Scott's body went limp.

'That wasn't very nice,' Robin said, snapping off his restraints and sitting up with a serious expression.

'You'll thank us when the meds wear off,' the male paramedic assured Robin. Then he turned around and spoke to the driver. 'Ísbjörg, let Control know we've got Robin on board and Officer Scott is out for the count.'

'Ísbjörg?' Robin said, as he shot a surprised glance over his shoulder. 'Ísbjörg! You look more beautiful than a tasty wheel of cheese.'

Ísbjörg took a little yellow walkie-talkie out of her fluorescent Locksley Ambulance Service jacket, but she couldn't use it because she was driving an ambulance at 160 kph and Robin had made her laugh.

'Robin, lie down!' the male paramedic ordered as he helped his colleague to disarm Scott and flop him back into the tilting chair. 'Your wounds won't close if you don't keep still.'

'K33, this is XR5,' Ísbjörg said when she finally stopped laughing. 'Police escort has been pacified. Make sure the quads are ready at the meeting point. We've got three drones and the Channel Seven chopper on our tail.'

# 47. HOME SWEET HOME

04:30

Little John woke with a jerk and took a second to figure out where he was. He looked out of the limo's bulletproof window. It was still dark and they were speeding down an empty Capital City street, with bus lanes, cycle lanes, sandwich shops and office blocks packed tight along either side.

'Eww,' he said, pushing his tongue around his parched mouth as he reached for a plastic water bottle.

'Ah, you're back with us,' Officer Catherine noted from the front seat. 'There's no traffic at this time of day. We'll be arriving in a few minutes.'

There was a large screen in front of the partition that separated John from the driver's compartment. He'd switched on a news channel after they'd dropped Clare at her house, and the ticker along the bottom of the screen said:

- ROBIN HOOD ARRESTED, ESCAPES IN STOLEN AMBULANCE.

'He escaped!' John said, gaping. 'Have you seen this?'

'I've been driving, so I'm not up to speed,' Catherine said. 'But Phuong called me when she found out what happened.'

John found a volume button for the screen and put the sound up. 'My mum will be punching holes in walls!' he said. 'So much for her positive headlines.'

'Scott won't be too happy either,' Catherine said.

'Is he OK?'

'Locksley police found Scott in the abandoned ambulance. Chained to the passenger seat with his own handcuffs. Nothing injured, except his pride.'

'That's good,' John said. 'He seems like a decent guy.'

'I'm impressed that the rebels got hold of an ambulance and put a sophisticated escape plan together so quickly,' Catherine said.

John thought for a second. 'I should have known something was up. Even on a normal day, when there hasn't been a riot, it's miraculous if a Locksley ambulance shows up in less than two hours.'

The news programme on the screen was showing two feeds. A big box on the left side ran a short clip on repeat. It was news drone footage of an ambulance parked at the edge of Sherwood Forest. Robin's stretcher was being rolled out of the back in near darkness, before a crew of rebels strapped it to a dirt bike trailer.

The smaller box on the right side of the screen showed a bespectacled pundit in a ludicrous bow tie. He sounded full of himself as he spoke about what Marjorie's presidential victory meant for the country. John was almost nodding off again when the newsreader asked for the pundit's thoughts on the election for Sheriff of Nottingham.

'Everyone was expecting Guy Gisborne to challenge Ardagh Hood's victory in the courts,' bow-tie man answered. 'Since the number of votes counted was higher than the number of people registered to vote, no serious person can deny that cheating took place.

'However, the Electoral Conduct Authority rules were designed to discourage frivolous challenges to election results. A result can only be challenged if a complaint is made by a losing candidate within forty-eight hours. Since Guy Gisborne passed away before lodging a complaint, I believe Ardagh Hood's position as the new Sheriff of Nottingham will stand.'

This made John smile, but it also made him think about his dad, and all the other people he loved.

Now she was president, would his mum deal as ruthlessly with Sherwood's rebels as she'd promised?

How would his dad cope with the everyday grind of being sheriff in one of the most deprived and corruption-riddled places in the country?

What was the atmosphere like at Clare's house, with her father dead and her mother and brothers knowing that she'd betrayed him in the final moments of his life?

Was Robin still loopy on pain meds? And would he get decent treatment in the rebel clinic at Sherwood Castle?

These thoughts got pushed aside as Catherine steered the armoured limousine under a grand arch and turned onto Presidential Drive.

The arrow-straight road was eight lanes wide. It stretched for a kilometre and a half, and had flagpoles down the middle. Government office buildings were set back in the surrounding parkland, and the colossal six-hundred-room Presidential Palace dazzled at the far end.

This was where John lived now.

Look out for the next

# ROBIN HOOD

**Read on for an extract . . .**

# 1. BLACK OR WHITE

The Three Sisters Canteen was decked out for the season, with strands of tinsel and a blinking-nosed inflatable reindeer. The café had been built to provide cheap breakfasts and rapid lunches to workers in car factories that no longer existed. Now, two-thirds of the tables were permanently roped off and the place survived serving hungover uni students and workers from Locksley's trash dumps.

Lottie the waitress seemed to have stepped from the past, with mountainous lacquered grey hair and frilly trim around her pink apron. Her eyes narrowed as she approached two fourteen-year-olds at a table close to the service counter.

'No school?' she asked, in a gravelly smoker's voice.

Josie Longshanks shook her head and told a lie. 'Dentist. We're due back after lunch.'

Lottie wasn't convinced because the pair were holding hands across the plastic table cover. But she wouldn't push it, as long as they were no trouble.

The boy was Alan Adale, Robin Hood's oldest friend. He was gangly and two metres tall, even with his afro squashed under a Nottingham Penguins baseball cap.

'Two cappuccinos,' Alan said.

Lottie got this from young people all the time and rolled her eyes as she pointed out a tall table with battered steel jugs. 'No fancy stuff here. Got bottomless black coffee and milk if you need it.'

Josie ordered tea and a bacon bap. Alan got coffee plus a fried-egg sandwich that burst with runny yolk when he took his first bite.

'Not my new shirt,' he whined, dabbing the stain with a napkin while Josie smirked.

As the pair ate, Christmas music on the radio broke for the hourly news. The two teens let the first story wash over them. Something about President Marjorie's PEPPA bill facing a crucial committee something or other. But the next item caught their ears.

*'Following yesterday's guilty verdicts, a judge in Locksley Superior Court has handed lengthy prison sentences to two Sherwood Forest rebels charged with terrorist and robbery offences. Nineteen-year-old Kevin 'Flash' Maid was sentenced to thirty-two years, while his eighteen-year-old partner Agnes McIntyre received twenty.'*

Alan and Josie were Sherwood rebels who knew Flash and Agnes, so the tough sentences gave them chills.

*'In other news, fire crews from as far as Capital City have been drafted into the Locksley area to try and contain a trash*

*dump fire that has been burning for three days. And Maddy the marmoset, who escaped from Capital City Zoo yesterday, has been safely returned to her enclosure. Now it's time for more festive tracks, here on Mellow Gold Radio . . .*

'Poor Flash,' Josie whispered, as she set her coffee mug down. 'Judge absolutely smashed them.'

'They'll only serve half, with good behaviour,' Alan noted, giving Josie's hand a reassuring squeeze.

'*Only* sixteen years,' Josie joked, waving a dismissive hand. 'No bother at all . . .'

Their gloomy thoughts were interrupted by Robin Hood's voice, crackling through the earpiece microphones they both wore. 'Our targets are parking up outside. Little electric Fiat. Custard yellow. Registration K—'

Alan glanced around to make sure nobody was close by before replying. 'Robin, you broke up after K. What's all that noise?'

'Rain,' Robin moaned. 'I'm on the roof and soaked through. Forget the registration. It's the little yellow car, right out front in the disabled bay.'

'Enjoy the rain, pal,' Alan told Robin, then looked up at Josie. 'It's on.'

It was hammering rain and the café windows had filthy net curtains, but Alan glanced casually sideways and viewed a comical scene as two obese goons squeezed out of the little car and charged through rain to the café entrance.

At the same time, Josie pulled a vape pod from the front pocket of her jeans and stood up.

'Need a quick puff,' she said, for the benefit of anyone nearby.

Josie swept by the two goons coming the other way. They were stereotypical thugs. Big necks, bigger guts, crude prison tattoos and bulky coats that hinted at weapons tucked beneath.

'Tell the boss we're here,' the taller of the two told a waitress, then leaned over a metal countertop next to the dumbwaiter that delivered plates from the basement kitchen.

Alan shifted in his seat, enough to see the goons without making it obvious that he was watching them. A sweat-glazed woman in a stained chef's apron came up from the basement kitchen and looked worried when she saw the goons at her service counter.

The canteen was too noisy for Alan to hear every word, but he caught the gist of what the goon snarled to the chef: *'Think you don't have to pay us now Mr Gisborne is dead?'*

Extortion rackets had been the backbone of Guy Gisborne's criminal empire. Whenever a new business started in the area, the owner would be approached by a couple of Gisborne's thugs and asked to pay a weekly fee for protection.

If the owner didn't cough up, staff got beaten, families threatened and premises were robbed, vandalised or burnt. And business owners who went to the cops soon learned that their complaints would be ignored, because most Locksley police officers were on Gisborne's payroll too.

'I already paid,' Alan heard the chef say desperately. 'There's no more. I can't even pay my meat supplier.'

Alan was witnessing a problem that now faced hundreds of Locksley businesses. When Guy Gisborne was Locksley's crime boss, everyone paid *his* thugs. Now Gisborne was dead, his organisation had split into rival factions, each claiming they had the right to rip off business owners.

While Alan watched the counter, Josie was out in the puddled parking lot. She didn't normally vape and felt self-conscious as she took a couple of puffs of peach-flavoured nicotine-free juice.

After glancing behind to make sure the two goons weren't coming out, she unzipped her little backpack, stepped up to the tiny yellow car and tapped her earpiece microphone to speak to Alan.

'There's no one around. Tell me the instant those guys head out.'

Alan kept one eye on the scared-looking chef as he answered. 'Boss lady is opening the till to give the goons some cash. You're safe, but hurry.'

'Roger that,' Josie said.

A big raindrop hit the back of Josie's neck, making her shudder as she took a small tracking device out of her pocket. Then she reached under the little Fiat's wheel arch and felt it snap on to the metal with a magnetic thump.

After looking around to make sure nobody was watching, Josie pulled out a second smaller device. It was dome-shaped and just 12 millimetres in diameter, but it contained a 360-degree camera and a microphone sensitive enough to let them hear what was being said inside the car.

Robin watched from the café roof and his voice bloomed in Josie's earpiece. 'Stick it on the tinted part at the bottom of the windscreen so they can't see it. But not where the wiper blade will catch it.'

Josie peeled off a strip of clear film to expose a sticky patch on the device's base, then tapped her earpiece.

'I know what I'm doing,' she answered irritably, simultaneously cleaning a corner of the windscreen with a napkin so the device would stick. 'It's on – test it.'

'Connected to my phone,' Robin confirmed. 'Only getting sound though. Wait . . . Now picture too.'

Josie took another puff on her vape as she backed away from the little Fiat. As she headed back inside, the chef had opened the cash register drawer and was handing cash to the goons.

Simultaneously, Alan had his nylon wallet out and trapped a twenty-pound note under his coffee mug to cover their bill.

'Wassup, beautiful?' the smaller of the two goons said, showing Josie a mouthful of yellow teeth and blatantly eyeing her up as she swept past.

Josie shuddered as she reached Alan. 'That bloke's breath smells like rotten fish.'

'Let's head out,' Alan told her. 'Got all your stuff?'

He caught Lottie the waitress's eye and pointed to the money he'd left on the table.

'I'll get your change,' Lottie said.

'Keep it,' Alan replied.

The titchy yellow Fiat reversed out of the disabled bay with the giant goons inside. As they drove off the lot, Josie led Alan back out into the rain. The pair jogged to the rear of the café building, where Robin had dropped from the café's flat roof, using the lid of a giant wheeled trash can as a step.

'You're a drowned rat!' Alan grinned, watching the rain trickle out of Robin's flattened hair.

Robin didn't see the funny side. 'Forty-five minutes squatting in a puddle.'

'And you missed our yummy breakfast,' Alan teased.

As Robin gave Alan the finger, Josie was already marching towards a trio of dirt bikes parked between the café and a hair salon.

'You two, stop winding each other up and get on your bikes,' she ordered. 'We'll lose connection to the spy cam if they get out of range.'

Robert Muchamore's books have sold
15 million copies in over 30 countries,
been translated into 24 languages and
been number-one bestsellers in eight
countries including the UK, France,
Germany, Australia and New Zealand.

Find out more at
muchamore.com

Follow Robert
on Facebook and Twitter
@RobertMuchamore

# Thank you for choosing a Hot Key book!

For all the latest bookish news, freebies and exclusive

content, sign up to the Hot Key newsletter – scan the

QR code or visit lnk.to/HotKeyBooks

## Follow us on social media:

**bonnierbooks.co.uk/HotKeyBooks**

## Robert Muchamore's ROBIN HOOD series

1. Hacking, Heists & Flaming Arrows
2. Piracy, Paintballs & Zebras
3. Jet Skis, Swamps & Smugglers
4. Drones, Dams & Destruction
5. Ransoms, Raids & Revenge
6. Bandits, Dirt Bikes & Trash
7. Prisons, Parties & Powerboats
8. Ballots, Blasts & Betrayal

*More ROBIN HOOD adventures to come!*